THE HE

‘I'm quite capable of running my own life without advice from *you*,’ Staff Nurse Nicky Pascall tells Dr Alex Baron. But if she is to recover from her broken heart, perhaps his tender loving care is the best way to start the healing process.

THE HEALING PROCESS

BY

GRACE READ

MILLS & BOON LIMITED
London · Sydney · Toronto

First published in Great Britain 1984
by Mills & Boon Limited, 15–16 Brook's Mews,
London W1A 1DR

Australian copyright 1984
Philippine copyright 1984

ISBN 0 263 74812 X

Set in 11 on 11½ pt Linotron Times
03–0884–48,500

Photoset by Rowland Phototypesetting Ltd
Bury St Edmunds, Suffolk
Made and printed in Great Britain by
Richard Clay (The Chaucer Press) Ltd
Bungay, Suffolk

CHAPTER ONE

THE IMPRESSIVE rose-brick facade of St Pancras station glowed in the sunshine of an early June afternoon. At a convenient set-down point a London taxi drew to a halt and discharged its two passengers, both girls in their early twenties.

Nicola, petite with shining brown shoulder-length hair, searched in her bag to settle the fare.

'I'll stay with this,' said her friend Elaine, standing by Nicola's bulging suitcase and handgrip. 'You go and get your ticket and check the time of the train.'

'OK, thanks.' Nicola hurried to the booking office, bought a single ticket and checked the departure board. 'I've got half an hour,' she said, returning to where her friend was waiting. 'The train's not even in yet. Shall we have a cup of coffee?'

'Yes, let's.'

Sitting on a bench within sight of the clock and the trains they sipped hot brown liquid from polystyrene beakers. Both were pensive and less chatty than usual.

'Good party last night,' Nicola said at length.

'Yes. Wish you hadn't decided to go and bury yourself in the Midlands though, Nicky.' Elaine chewed her lip regretfully. 'You could have got a staff nurse's job somewhere nearer, for goodness sake.'

Both girls had passed their SRN in March, along with a goodly proportion of the rest of their set at the Royal Heathside Hospital. Elaine was staying on there as a staff nurse. Being unofficially engaged to Dr Simon Hill, the obstetrics registrar, she naturally wished to stay near him. Nicola had decided to move on, saying that she wanted to widen her experience, but her true reason she had confided to no one.

Elaine's boyfriend was as charming a rat as it was possible to find, was Nicola's opinion. Over the past months she had been increasingly worried by his attentions to her when Elaine was out of the way. Even if they did eventually marry, Simon was not cut out to be the faithful type. But no way was Nicola going to be responsible for any break-up of the romance.

She didn't even particularly like Simon, which seemed to make him all the more keen. She was a notch to his belt that he had to have. The only solution Nicola could see was to take herself off the scene. But now that the time for parting had come she was regretful at the thought of leaving her old circle of friends.

'Come up and see me, won't you?' she said. 'It's barely a couple of hours by train. We can go to Stratford and catch up on some culture. And there's some lovely countryside around.'

'I know. I come from Derbyshire, remember? You can always go and see my folks if you're at a loose end.'

'Maybe I will, if I get desperate . . . although it's a good way from Priory Cross.'

The hands of the station clock moved on to five.

A voice over the air announced that passengers for Leicester could now take their seats on the train.

'I'm not going to enjoy living in a nurses' home again,' groaned Nicola, pulling her heavy suitcase along the platform on its inset wheels. They searched for a suitable compartment. 'It's been great for the past eighteen months, sharing the flat with you. Hope Ros fits in all right.'

'Well, it won't be quite the same as it was with us. But anyway,' Elaine went on brightly, 'I'm hoping I shan't be there too much longer myself, if only I can pin Simon down to a date. He says he doesn't want to make any definite plans until he's got the next part of his gynae membership.'

They had stopped outside a non-smoking section of the train where there seemed to be plenty of room. 'This will do me,' Nicola said, heaving her luggage aboard and moving along the corridor to find an empty compartment.

Between them they pushed her suitcase beneath the seat and secured her place by the window with her handgrip. 'Sorry I've had to leave so much stuff behind, but I'll be back for it as soon as I can, tell Ros. I'd better get something to read,' she went on.

Further along the platform there was a portable magazine stand. Nicola chose a weekly magazine and a nursing periodical, after which the girls stood talking until the guard came along slamming doors. Boarding the train, Nicola shut the door and leaned out of the window, her nut-brown hair falling silkily about her small symmetrical features. 'Thanks for coming,' she said with a sigh.

Elaine spread her hands in a resigned gesture. 'Give me a ring soon and let's know how you get on.' She grinned. 'Just think, a whole new field of talent to choose from. And the hospital's just as modern as the Heathside, isn't it, so it should be a nice place to work in!'

The whistle blew and the train began to pull away. The girls waved to each other; then Elaine turned for the barrier and Nicola made her way along the corridor to her compartment.

Two other people had taken their seats since she had reserved her own. In the opposite window seat there was a plump middle-aged woman in a fawn Crimplene suit and a fawn straw beret. In the opposite corner nearest the corridor sprawled an athletically-built man, busily engaged in some lengthy writing project. His long, muscular legs, encased in grubby jeans and terminating in dusty brown moccasins, were stretched out across the entrance, blocking her way.

'Excuse me, please,' said Nicola with a tentative smile in his direction.

He pulled his feet in at once to let her pass, giving her no more than a fleeting glance, but for a second their eyes met. His eyes, she noticed, were strikingly blue, set deep between darkish curling lashes. His wealth of dark-blond hair had been bleached in places by the sun and a rich strand of it fell across his broad forehead.

Outdoors type, Nicola absently labelled him. Slinging her lightweight rain-jacket up on the rack, she settled herself in her seat and opened the weekly magazine. Turning the pages idly, she began to read about the exploits of a famous film star, but it was less than absorbing and her thoughts constantly strayed, remembering the life she was leaving behind. They had been great times on the whole . . . apart from that disastrous period after she had learned about Leo. Her fellow students had been more like the sisters she had never had. Cutting herself off from them was like losing a whole family at one fell swoop. *Damn you, Simon*, she thought to herself.

The woman in the seat opposite had been eating a bar of chocolate, but now she rummaged in her shopping bag, found a packet of cigarettes and took a lighter from her handbag. She lit up and inhaled with deep satisfaction before letting out a stream of smoke. As it wafted across towards her, Nicola glanced at the No Smoking sign on the window. The woman caught her eye. 'Don't mind, do you?' she said carelessly.

With a non-committal shrug Nicola returned to her reading.

'But I'm afraid I do, madam,' spoke up a deep, resolute voice from the opposite corner. 'I'd be obliged if you'd either put that out or finish it in the corridor.'

It was an ultimatum. The woman snorted, glared at the flaxen-haired giant like an outraged hen, picked up her packages and, with the cigarette hanging from her lips, stormed out of the carriage.

She left the door wide open. Without a word he closed it after her with one easy movement of his long arm.

Nicola curbed a smile. 'Thank you,' she said, 'I wouldn't have dared to complain.'

Her companion was clearly not in the mood for polite small talk. He gazed at her steadily for a moment, as though really seeing her for the first time. 'Then I suggest you start daring, unless you enjoy being walked over.' Unsmiling, he returned to writing on the large pad which he was resting on an expensive-looking brief-case. But she caught the hint of amusement which crossed his strong, angular features.

Self-opinionated clown, she thought, and decided the best course was to ignore him. Discarding her woman's magazine she turned to the nursing periodical and endeavoured to concentrate on an article on total hip replacement.

At Priory Cross Hospital Nicola was to be staffing on an orthopaedic ward with a view to taking the specialised course later. It had been Simon's unwelcome attentions that first prompted her to make the change. Now she was beginning to get cold feet and to wonder if she had been a fool, letting Simon drive her away.

With her parents at present living in America, where her father had transferred for his firm, she had no home base other than an aunt living somewhere in Suffolk. Quite suddenly she felt like an abandoned orphan and stupidly her eyes smarted with tears. Sniffing, she blinked them back, turning to look out of the carriage window so that the other occupant of the compartment should not see.

They had left the city behind by now. Green fields rushed by. The warm quiet of the late afternoon was broken only by the rumble of the train. With the window half open, the scent of summer wafted in on the breeze. It brought with it memories of buttercup fields, waist-high when she was a child, and long idyllic days when all there had been to worry about was being chosen for the netball team or who you would have for maths next term.

But that was long before Leo. Before she had known the pleasure and pain of love and the events that had shattered her illusions. *Leo, why, oh why, did you do it? If only I'd known . . . we might have worked something out.* But she hadn't known, until it was too late.

As she relived moments of anguish the tears were there again, threatening to overflow. She searched in her handbag for a tissue and again in the pocket of her red jeans without success, and so she continued to sniff stealthily, smoothing away the tears with her fingers.

Her fellow traveller glanced across with a look of pained forbearance. 'Don't you have a handkerchief?' he demanded.

She swallowed and blinked at him through misty green eyes. 'Y-yes . . . I have, somewhere . . .'

'Well, I wish you'd blow your nose and stop sniffing. I'm trying to concentrate,' he said with some irritation.

Nicola's normally even temper snapped. 'It only says No Smoking . . . I can't see No Sniffing anywhere,' she retorted. 'I can't help it if I've got a cold. Go somewhere else if it annoys you!'

Jumping up from her seat she pulled down her jacket from the rack, found a handkerchief in the pocket and blew her nose noisily.

His eyebrows rose eloquently. 'I thought you implied you couldn't say boo to a goose?'

'I meant I prefer not to make scenes,' she returned with dignity. 'Get on with your wretched scribbling and I'll try not to spread my germs.'

The penetrating blue eyes held hers for a moment. She knew they saw through her pretend cold and she looked down at her magazine, trying to concentrate on her reading. At least the diversion had helped her to snap out of her mood, and from time to time she observed him covertly. With her eyes still a little misty she sought to size him up.

Through her damp lashes he seemed to glow like some Nordic sun god, lounging in the corner with his bright head bent over his writing. Or perhaps he was more akin to a Viking warrior—the kind who would have laid seige to the girl of his desire, carried her off and had his way with her. But only after he'd wooed and won her, of course, she thought with a private smile at her own fantasising. She'd been reading too many historical novels!

In spite of his casual, somewhat soiled appearance, there was an air of class about the man. The fawn sweater over his blue-checked shirt had the mark of quality, although grubby. His hands and nails were clean and well-kept, not the hands of a workman. He wore an expensive gold wrist-watch and he was writing with a gold ballpoint. She was curious to know more about him. He certainly appeared to have everything going for him, except tolerance, the belligerent brute.

Presently he put his work away in the smart brief-case and glanced at his watch. She glanced at hers. There was still an hour before they would reach Leicester and she smothered a yawn.

A white-jacketed waiter pushed open the door. 'Tea now being served in the buffet car,' he announced, and moved on.

Her companion rose. 'Come on, I'll buy you some tea, by way of a peace-pipe,' he said.

'Thank you. I should hate to be on your conscience.'

He ushered her through the door without touching her but she could feel his vital presence close behind her as they made for the buffet car. Sitting opposite her he eyed her lazily, evidently aware of her unspoken curiosity about his appearance. 'Yes, sorry about my tatty gear . . . I don't usually entertain ladies in this condition.'

'Why, what happened to you?' she asked.

'I was getting to grips with a car.'

'Oh, a breakdown?'

'Not mine, someone else's. But while I was being a good Samaritan my own car got pinched, which left me stranded like this.'

'I see. Does that account for you biting my head off, or are you always short on civility?'

He pushed over the plate of biscuits and again she noticed his well-kept but capable hands. 'I admit to feeling put out,' he said. 'As well as my car and luggage I lost a very valuable set of papers that took me forever to put together. Anyway, biting your head off, if that's what I did, helped to take your mind off your own problems, didn't it? You don't really have a cold.'

There was something disarming about the stranger and she grinned at him. 'That's my story and I'm sticking to it.'

'OK, I'll mind my own business. Just so long as you don't think you've got a monopoly on disasters. We all have our hang-ups—even that dear lady who was trying to poison our lungs as well as her own.'

Nicola's green eyes widened. 'Quite the philosopher, aren't you? I'll try to remember that next time I'm tempted to sound off at anyone who's rude to me.'

'It gets easier with practice,' he returned with a satirical twist to his shapely lips.

'So when are you going to start practising . . . and what's your own particular hang-up?'

'To your first point, I don't necessarily follow my own good advice; to your second, inquisitive females.'

They continued sparring with each other without real animosity. In fact Nicola quite enjoyed pitting her wits against his and the rest of the journey passed quickly.

Arriving at Leicester, he helped her pull her suitcase from under the seat and carried it to the ticket-barrier. 'Sorry I can't offer you a lift. Can you manage now?'

'Yes, thanks. I shall get a taxi.'

'Right. Goodbye then.' He held out his hand and the warm pressure of it, clasping hers, sent an odd little thrill down her spine. 'Perhaps we shall bump into each other again,' he said.

'You never know,' she returned, although she thought it hardly likely. 'Goodbye.'

For a moment she watched his lithe form weaving its way athletically through the dispersing crowds. His burnished head stood out amongst varying shades of brown and she experienced a twinge of regret that a fascinating personality had walked out of her life. But at least it had proved one thing, she reflected optimistically, there *were* other interesting characters beyond the world she had left behind. It rested with her to make the most of her new environment.

Nicola hailed a taxi to take her to the hospital which lay out towards the north-west. As they drove through the city she glanced about her with interest. It seemed to be a lively, go-ahead place with plenty of good shops. There was a vast open-air market and interesting little side streets with decorative lampposts. Modern multi-storey buildings vied with well-preserved reminders of the city's past.

Presently they left the city behind, passing through less congested residential areas and arriving at last at Priory Cross Hospital in its green surroundings. After paying off the taxi, Nicola reported to the warden of the nurses' home. She was shown up to her room on the fourth floor.

'This is really the sisters' floor,' the warden explained, 'but we've had to put a few staff nurses up here. You'll find the kitchen and bathrooms and laundry room at the end of the corridor. And there's a TV room down that way,' she pointed. 'If you don't want to cook for yourself there's a canteen on the ground floor, but it's finished for tonight. You could still get something over at the hospital canteen though.'

'Thank you,' said Nicola.

'And don't forget to keep your valuables locked up,' the warden advised. 'With so many people coming and going we can't be responsible.'

Left to her own devices Nicola took stock of her room. It was usefully furnished with a lockable wardrobe, writing-desk, dressing-table, wash-basin fitment and mirror. The divan bed had a green folk-weave coverlet to match the curtains at the window. On the bed were her new white uniforms and the frilly-edged caps of her staff nurse's status.

The room was stuffy. Pushing open the window Nicola looked across the sweep of green lawns towards the hospital buildings. The original ancient grey-stoned priory, now used for administrative purposes, stood dwarfed by the modern hospital layout that had risen around it.

At eight o'clock it was still quite light and she watched the passage of humanity flowing in and out of the place on this warm June evening. There were visitors arriving and departing, strings of food trolleys being shunted back to the kitchens, white-coated personnel walking purposefully in various directions and ambulances waiting outside the impressive Accident and Emergency department.

It was rather like being parachuted into alien territory, Nicola mused. All very confusing at first sight. Possibly within a week she would know her way around, but how long it would be before she really felt at home was another matter. For the time being she felt very much like the only new girl in the school. Well, that was what she had wanted, a fresh start, so there was no point in being faint-hearted.

In her handgrip Nicola had packed a few provisions. She took out her jar of coffee and a mug and went along to the kitchen to make a drink before starting to unpack. Stirring something in a saucepan on the stove was a large woman in a padded, floral-nylon dressing-gown. Her hair was short, thick and iron-grey, neatly cut. She swivelled sharp grey eyes in Nicola's direction and said bluntly, 'This is the sisters' kitchen, dear!'

The accent was broad Scots and the tone less than welcoming. It reminded Nicola of her days as a first-year when she had gone in awe of anyone with a navy blue dress or even belt. Inside she quailed . . . until the words of her companion in the train suddenly came back to her. *I suggest you start daring, unless you want to be walked over.*

So she smiled pleasantly and said, 'Good evening. Yes, I do know, but the warden said I should use it as I'm living on this floor.' Going to the sink she filled the kettle and plugged it in, adding, 'I'm Nicola Pascall. I'm just starting here.'

'Sister Flint,' returned the other woman. 'Which ward are you on?'

'I'm staffing on Montfort . . . Orthopaedics.'

'Oh, I see,' Sister Flint sniffed. 'Well, kindly remember, nobody's allowed more than one pint of milk, two eggs and a half-pound of butter in this fridge. And don't leave food about in your room. We don't want to encourage mice.'

'Oh dear, do we have those?' Nicola murmured.

'Not yet, but we shall have if you young gurrls aren't more careful.' Sister Flint poured her oatmeal porridge into a dish and put the saucepan to soak. 'Where did you train?'

'The Royal Heathside.'

A raised eyebrow and pursed lips greeted this information. 'The London gurrls think they know it all, but you'll find the provinces are just as efficient.'

'I'm sure they are,' agreed Nicola. She made her coffee and said goodnight, not wanting to be drawn into an argument, but she fervently hoped that Sister Flint was not typical of all the sisters at Priory Cross. It was not an encouraging introduction.

Later, having finished her unpacking, she went along to have a bath, and bumped into a girl of about her own age coming out of the laundry room with an armful of freshly-ironed clothes. Soft fair hair drifted about the shoulders of her tightly fitting navy T-shirt and her eyes were china-blue. At around five foot five she was slightly taller than Nicola.

'Hi!' she said brightly, pausing. 'You living on this floor?'

'Yes, I've only just arrived.'

'Welcome to the nunnery. I'm fairly new myself. Doing my midder. My name's Iris.'

'I'm Nicky Pascall. I'm the new staff nurse on Montfort.'

'Oh, poor you,' said Iris. 'They say Sister Cromwell is about as good as a sick headache.'

Nicola groaned. 'I just met a Sister Flint in the kitchen, and she wasn't exactly inspiring either.'

Iris rolled her eyes. 'She's Sister ITU. Rumour has it she can do cardiac massage with one hand and direct the entire ward with the other! By the way, she treats the TV room as her own private property. If you want to watch anything special I've a small black and white set in my room, so feel free. Room sixteen.'

'Oh, thanks,' smiled Nicola. 'It's nice to meet one friendly face anyway. I'm in fifteen.'

'Yes, thought you might be. That's directly opposite me. Been empty for a couple of weeks. Flint's further down, thank goodness. See you around.' With a cheerful grin she went on her way.

Feeling bucked after Iris's more friendly approach, Nicola went on to have her bath. But she couldn't help puzzling over what Iris had meant about Sister Cromwell being a 'sick headache'. Although it was customary to be seen by the ward sister when being interviewed for the job, Sister Cromwell had been away at the time and so they had yet to meet. Again her travelling companion's philosophy came to the rescue. Maybe Sister Cromwell also had her hang-ups. And it was pointless to go by gossip; it was best to make up your own mind about people.

In the corridor there was a communal pay phone. Before going to bed Nicola phoned her old London flat to give Elaine her number. It was Simon who answered. He held a flirtatious conversation with her before passing her over. 'Missing me yet?' he asked.

'I haven't had time to breathe, let alone miss anyone. First impressions are great. I thought I'd better let Elaine have my phone number, in case she needed to get in touch.'

'Ah, you wait till the novelty wears off,' he warned, 'you'll be wishing you had dear Simon's shoulder to cry on.'

'Not planning to do any crying, *dear* Simon,' she retorted, 'and I'm choosy over shoulders, as you well know.'

He chuckled, and with a feeling of distaste she pictured his wily, self-satisfied face, the sensuous lips and calculating dark eyes, and wondered why on earth Elaine put up with him.

'Remind me to spank you for that remark,' he said. 'I may be up your way sometime. Just remembered there's a mate of mine at Priory Cross. Joe Lismore, in Radiology. You may run across him.'

'Yes, maybe. Now, if you wouldn't mind passing me over to Elaine . . .'

She had wanted to have a heart-to-heart with her friend about feeling isolated and missing the old crowd, but having given the opposite impression to Simon she had to go on pretending that everything was marvellous. 'As soon as I find out when I've got days off I'll let you know, then I'll be back to collect the rest of my stuff,' she concluded, more positively than she felt.

Up early the following morning and not having to report until midday, Nicola caught a bus into the city, bought a few provisions and window-shopped. She liked the atmosphere of the place; there was a country tranquility about it despite its twentieth-century industry and commercialism and she felt she would enjoy discovering the history of the city when she had more time.

Buying a ready-made pack of sandwiches, she took them back to her room and ate them while changing into her uniform. With her hair neatly coiled up under her cap, navy belt fitting snugly about her small waist, training school badge and fob watch pinned one on either side of her white dress, she was ready to report to Mrs Young, the Senior Nursing Officer, as instructed.

'I'm glad to see you've put your hair up, Nurse,' said Mrs Young approvingly. 'Some of the newer students are very untidy these days. I like trained staff to set them a good example.'

Montfort Ward was on the ground floor of the west wing. Mrs Young conducted Nicola along to introduce her to Sister Cromwell. Nicola was agreeably surprised to find the sister a comparatively young person, possibly in her mid-thirties. She was tall, dark-haired, rather too thin, and giving the impression of being super-efficient, even when replacing a white hairclip in her diminutive pillbox cap.

She rose from her desk to greet her new staff nurse and when the nursing officer had left them, invited Nicola to sit down while she explained the workings of the ward.

'You know, I suppose, that we're a mixed ward? Alternate male and female four-bedded units.'

'Yes,' said Nicola. 'I think that's rather nice and the patients still have their privacy, don't they?'

'Yes. We usually have two SRN's, two SEN's and two or three students on each shift. But we've been short of permanent trained staff lately. I'd better take you through the Kardex, so you'll have some idea of the patients,' she went on rapidly. 'Have you done much orthopaedics?'

'I've been acting staff nurse on a male orthopaedic ward for the past four months.'

'Oh, good. It's such a nuisance when you have to spell things out to people. I like to leave my staff to get on with the job without too much supervision. There's quite enough for me to do with administration.' She fiddled with her cap again. 'I expect you'll find differences here from your last place. You know consultants and their pet theories, but you'll soon pick up their fads, and our senior registrar Alex Baron is pretty sane. His houseman

Max O'Malley knows his stuff, too. They'll be round later this afternoon, so we'd better get on.'

She skimmed through the Kardex notes like lightning, giving Nicola scarcely time to take anything in. 'You can gen up properly on their case histories later,' she said with a careless wave of her hand. 'Now, you understand we work internal rotation here . . . one month night duty in every four. All except me, I don't do nights.' She broke off as a buxom third-year student looked in at the doorway. 'Yes, Meryl?'

'Had I better do the drugs, Sister? Sophie isn't back from lunch yet.'

'The drugs? Oh, yes.' Sister Cromwell reached into her pocket for the keys and handed them to Nicola. 'You might as well start on that then. This is Nurse Ferry,' she went on. 'She'll show you where we keep the trolley and go round with you. All right?'

'Yes, Sister. Where do I put my things?'

'In the locker behind you,' Sister Cromwell said with a jerk of her head. 'Now I must get down to this stock requisition.'

Nicola deposited her bag on a shelf in the cupboard, smiled at the third-year and followed her out into the ward. 'Call me Nicky,' she said, 'and you're Meryl, did Sister say?'

'Yes, that's right.' Nurse Ferry's round, pink face creased into a smile. She led the way to where the drugs trolley was stationed. 'Are you permanent?'

'I hope so.'

'Oh, good. We've had a whole string of agency staff lately, and it's not the same. Do you want me to dispense, or will you?'

'You'd better do it since you know the patients, I'll check,' said Nicola, deciding to tread gently.

The patients ranged from teenagers with limbs damaged in road accidents, to the elderly with fractured neck-of-femurs, sportsmen with back and cartilage problems, industrial injuries and short-stay patients for minor surgery. Taking medication sheets from the various headboards gave Nicola time to glance at temperature charts and the chance to introduce herself.

Apart from the mixed sexes, the work was much the same as she had been doing in London. There were the same sand-bagged limbs and plaster bandages, spinal beds and traction weights, and physiotherapists putting patients through their exercises. It did not take her long to feel at home. She was soon chatting away to the patients in her usual friendly fashion.

By the time the round was completed and they had locked the trolley back in position Nicola felt she was going to like Meryl, who it appeared was shortly to be taking her Finals.

'And the more I swot, the less I seem to know,' she despaired. 'I bet I don't get any of the things I've revised.'

'Oh, everyone feels like that,' Nicola reassured her. 'I expect you'll be all right. The main thing is not to panic.'

'Panic? Nobody panics on my ward, Staff,' put in Sister Cromwell, catching the comment as she came from checking the Dangerous Drugs cupboard.

'We were talking about my Finals, Sister,' put in Meryl.

'Oh, was that all? Well, will you take one of the others and make sure the ward is tidy. We'll have the doctors with us soon. Oh, here they come now,' she added, turning at the sound of activity through the ward doors. 'Better forget that for the time being and bring the notes trolley, Meryl. You come with me, er, Nicola, isn't it?' She went forward to meet the party with Nicola following in her wake.

The houseman, Max O'Malley, was a small merry-eyed Irishman with a dark beard. He smiled at them all. Also in the party were the physio-therapist and a medical student, but it was the fourth member of the group who caused Nicola's eyes to widen and her stomach to flip. It was the sun-god—in a white coat. Blond hair gleaming and smartly brushed, dark blue eyes showing mild amusement, he caught her own dumbstruck expression.

'Good afternoon, Alex,' Sister Cromwell flapped, repinning her cap. 'This is Staff Nurse Pascall. She has just joined us.'

'How do you do?' said Nicola's travelling companion with a slight bow. 'I hope you're going to enjoy working here.'

Nicola gulped. 'Thank you, sir. I'm sure I shall.'

So *he* was the senior orthopaedic registrar. Oh help! If only she'd known!

Following the circus around the ward she had difficulty keeping her mind on the job, unable to forget the unfortunate nature of their first meeting. She had probably left him with the impression that she was a spineless cry-baby. She might lack confidence in certain areas of her private life, it was true, but that certainly did not apply to her work.

With a determined effort Nicola concentrated on taking in the details of each patient being discussed. She knew she was a good nurse, so she decided to set about proving it to that smart alec straight-away . . .

CHAPTER TWO

HAVING collected her lunch-time ham salad from the canteen counter, Nicola looked around for a seat.

'Come and sit with us, Nicky,' called Staff Nurse Sophie Dakin.

Nicola had noticed the lively West Indian girl sitting with her friends, but had not liked to butt in. It was her second day on Montfort Ward and she had worked only briefly with Sophie the previous afternoon. Now she gladly accepted the invitation.

Sophie was also fairly new to the ward but she had trained at Priory Cross and therefore knew a great many people. She introduced the other girls, both staff nurses. 'This is Hannah and this is Louise.'

'How're you getting on with our Dora?' Louise wanted to know.

'We-ell,' said Nicola with a hesitant smile, 'so far so good. I've met worse. She certainly doesn't interfere much.'

'Except when Alex Baron's around,' giggled Sophie. 'She's nuts about him. But then, who isn't?'

It hadn't taken Nicola long to discover why Sister Dora Cromwell had the reputation of being a 'sick headache'. Her show of being an efficient whirl-wind was that and no more. She appeared to be incapable of making decisions. If she gave an order with one breath she was likely to change her mind with the next. She left the running of the ward to the staff nurses while busying herself with the office work. Not that Nicola minded. You knew where you were if you were left to get on with the job. But it seemed indiscreet at this stage to pass her opinion, and she was glad when conversation veered away from ward talk.

'Miss Willis—she's our social secretary,' Hannah explained, 'wants money-raising ideas for the garden fête at the end of the month.'

'Fancy asking nurses for money-raising ideas,' giggled Sophie. 'Now, if they asked us how to spend it . . .'

'Where do they hold that?' asked Nicola.

'Behind the tennis-courts at the back of the hospital. It's run by the Friends' League really, but they like some nurses in uniform to lend a bit of atmosphere. They had me on the "Tip-the-nurse-out-of-bed" booth last year,' said Louise, ruefully rubbing her backside. 'They can find another volunteer for that! I'll go on something soft like the book stall.'

Their lunch finished, Nicola and Sophie went back to the ward together. Nicola had been on duty since seven-thirty, but at one o'clock Sophie was just reporting for her late shift. 'Anything spectacular happened since yesterday?' she asked.

'No. Oh! Yes, old Mrs Yelverton did a spectacular, stripping naked in the middle of visitors last night.'

Sophie let out a peal of laughter. 'She does that regularly, poor love. She'll be going back to her old folks' home soon, now that her hip's fixed.'

Sister Cromwell went off for her half-day when the staff nurses reported back, and the girls sorted out the work between them. Sophie and Meryl did the drugs round while Nicola and Karen Rees, a capable enrolled nurse, helped patients back to bed in time for visitors.

There were twenty-eight patients for Nicola to get to know as well as her new workmates, but by making herself generally useful she had no difficulty in finding acceptance. Compared with some wards the patients on Montfort were predominantly cheerful. Once they had recovered from the initial shock of accident or surgery, they were more incapacitated than ill.

Coming to their youngest patient, pretty sixteen-year-old Avril Jenkins, Nicola and Karen made her comfortable and rearranged her pillows. 'Would you like to change your nightie?' Nicola asked.

Avril nodded and mouthed, 'Pink one.'

Avril aroused everyone's compassion. She was on traction with a difficult compound fracture of the tibia after being involved in a motor bike accident.

Her boyfriend, who had been driving, was in the neurosurgical ward, still unconscious after two weeks. And the shock of it all had robbed Avril of the power to speak. She made herself understood by writing on a pad, but she was altogether too subdued for Nicola's liking.

'Your mum coming this afternoon?' Karen asked the girl as they helped her into her clean nightdress.

Avril nodded apathetically.

'Well, let's comb your hair and make you look nice,' said Nicola. She found a comb in the locker and eased a tangle out of the long fair hair, being careful not to pull around the damaged side of Avril's face. 'There, that's better, and you'll soon be able to put some make-up on. Want to see?' She held out a small hand mirror. Avril looked and made a face at her grazes. Both nurses laughed but as they moved on to their next patient they exchanged pitying looks.

Later, at the end of visiting, Avril's mother sought out Nicola for a word. 'How do you think she is, Nurse?'

'She's making satisfactory progress, Mrs Jenkins, except for the voice problem, but that will take time. Is she usually a quiet sort of girl, I mean, apart from not being able to speak at the moment?'

'Good Lord, no,' her mother said, 'she was just a normal lively teenager. I've never known her like this. If only we could give her some good news of Brian, that would perk her up. But he just lies there. They were potty about each other—they were getting married in September . . .' She bit her trembling lips, not able to go on.

Nicola felt her own throat tighten, but she spoke encouragingly. 'Well, try not to let her see you're worried. There's no reason why Avril shouldn't do well.'

It was easy enough to give advice, but Nicola knew that the reality was very different. Shattered lives took a long time to heal.

In charge of the ward the following day, she had to call Dr O'Malley about a rise in Avril's temperature and some offensive discharge from the wound over the site of the fracture.

'Wretched motor bikes,' he fumed in the office

when he had written the girl up for a further course of antibiotics. 'They should be banned from the road.'

'You might as well try to ban breathing, Dr O'Malley,' she returned.

'Yes, I suppose so. The name's Max, by the way. And how are you liking yourself here?'

'Oh, fine. It'll be better when I get to know some more people. I'm a bit lost off duty. I'm a long way from my old friends.'

'London, wasn't it?'

'Yes. Actually I travelled down in the same carriage as Mr Baron last Sunday, although I didn't know who he was at the time.'

Max stroked his curly black beard. 'Ah yes, lost his car that weekend. And all his notes for this thesis he's writing on spinal injuries, poor guy. Well, keep encouraging young Avril to talk, won't you?'

Nicola walked with him to the door. 'She was planning to get married in the autumn, her mother told me.'

'That's life!' sighed Max. 'Look, why don't you drop in at the Nun's Head tonight? That's where a lot of us migrate after work. Will I look out for you?'

'Well, thanks. Maybe I'll come some time, but not tonight,' Nicola said. 'I'm here until nine-thirty and after that I've got a few things to do.'

Sister Cromwell had given her Saturday and Sunday off, and back at the nurses' home that night Nicola phoned Elaine. This time they managed to have a private conversation, Simon not being there.

'I've got the weekend off,' Nicola announced, 'but I'm on a late on Friday so I shan't be coming up till Saturday morning. There's a train gets in about ten . . . I'll be with you by half-past.'

'Oh good,' returned Elaine. 'I'm working Saturday morning, but I'm off in the afternoon. Don't know about Ros, but if she's on duty we'll leave the key in the usual place. How're you doing? What's it like up there?'

'I haven't had much time to find out yet,' said Nicola. 'Met a girl named Iris the first night I was here. She lives opposite me, but I haven't seen her since. There's a dragon of a sister who lives along the corridor. I was invited over to the local by one of the housemen tonight, but I was too whacked to go.'

Elaine tutted. 'You've got to make the effort, Nicky. Going back to your room every night will get you nowhere.'

'Don't bully me! One of these days I'll surprise you.' The pips went. 'No more money,' said Nicola. 'See you Saturday, then. Bye.'

She had cheered up considerably since her earlier phone call, but she was really looking forward to going back to her old haunts. Returning to her room, she collected her mug and a plate and went along to the kitchen to scramble an egg for her supper. In the middle of her cooking efforts Sister Flint appeared on the scene.

Wearing her usual floral dressing-gown, she was hot and bothered and extremely weary. With a casual nod in Nicola's direction she went to the fridge for her carton of milk. Opening it, she sniffed at it suspiciously and let out an exclamation of annoyance. 'Oh! Would you believe it! That's off! And it was only yesterday I bought it.'

Nicola looked sympathetic. 'Must be the thundery weather. Have some of mine . . . it's long-life.' She passed over her own carton.

'Thank you, lass.' Sister Flint's expression warmed a little. 'It won't leave you short for the morning?'

'Oh, that's all right. I'm not on until midday, I can always go down to the canteen.'

'Verra guid of you. I'll pay you back.'

'Forget it,' said Nicola. She thought the woman looked dispirited. 'Did you have a busy day?' she asked.

'Lost two of my patients. A salutary reminder of human limitations in spite of technical advances. Makes one feel inadequate. Can't go around weeping for everyone, but it still affects you.'

Nicola saw the woman with new insight. She was holding down a responsible and traumatic job, probably coming back to a lonely existence at the nurses' home. No one to share her burdens with . . . it was enough to make anyone crabby. 'It must be heart-breaking for you sometimes,' she said.

But Sister Flint was not one to allow herself to indulge in sentiment. She changed the subject. 'You're on Montfort, you said? I'll be putting my feet up there as soon as Mr Tresilian can fit me in. Alex Baron says it's high time I had my hallux valgus done. I suppose he's right.'

Glancing down at the woman's feet in her flat, foam-padded slippers, Nicola recognised the ugly big-toe joints on both of them. 'Oh, you've got bunions! Well, it'll be a good thing to have done, won't it?'

'Hmm!' Sister Flint pursed her lips. 'Can't say I'm looking forward to it. Never been a patient myself before, but I expect I'll survive.'

I hope *we* shall! brooded Nicola, carrying her meal back to her room. The prospect of having Sister Flint as a patient was somewhat daunting. Every move of the nurses would be under her critical eye. It would be like having practical ward assessments all over again. Sister Cromwell couldn't care less about little details like mitred bed-corners so long as on the surface everything looked all right. Sister Flint, on the other hand, would probably judge them with eyes like set squares.

The following morning after the report Sister Cromwell said, 'I'll leave you to allocate the work, Nicola, I've got all these path lab reports to deal with.'

'OK, Sister.' Thursday was theatre day and Nicola ran her finger down the operation list. 'Who needs prepping? There's Gil Stevens for his meniscectomy . . . his leg will need shaving. By the way, I hear Sister Flint is to come in soon to have her bunions done.'

Dora Cromwell clutched her brow and groaned. 'Oh, no! Where did you hear that?'

'We live on the same floor in the nurses' home. She told me Mr Baron wants to fit her in as soon as possible.'

'Oh well, I've got some holiday owing to me. With any luck I shan't be here.'

Nicola detailed the staff to their various tasks and

asked Karen to help her bed-bath Tom Woodman, a miner with a fractured pelvis and a bladder injury, who needed careful handling.

'I bet you anything you like, as soon as she knows when Sister ITU's coming in, she'll be off!' prophesied Karen darkly as she put a bowl of water and a mouthwash on a trolley.

'Can't say I blame her,' Nicola laughed, placing a clean sheet on the bottom shelf.

They wheeled the trolley to Tom's bedside and gave him their attention. He had been in for ten days since the pit accident. He was making good progress but was still immobilised, with his pelvis in a sling attached to a Balkan beam. Although married he was a shy man, acutely embarrassed at not being able to do much for himself. By talking cheerfully about TV programmes and other matters while they washed him and treated his pressure areas, they managed to take his mind off their attentions.

'We should get the all-clear for your stitches to come out today, Tom,' Nicola said, tucking in her side of the clean bottom sheet.

'Then shall I be able to come down off this contraption?' he asked.

'Probably. It depends on your latest X-ray. The doctors will be up to see you later. Keep drinking, won't you? Good for your bladder. Two of those jugs a day, at least.'

'Strewth. I'll burst me bloody stitches if you have your way, Staff,' he grinned.

Swishing back the bed curtains, Nicola looked across at Tom's immediate neighbour. Gil Stevens, due for his cartilage operation that day, was sitting by his bed. He was a footballer and a local hero. 'Have you had a bath this morning, Gil?' Nicola asked him.

'Yes love, I'm as sweet as you are,' he returned cheekily. 'What time am I for the chop?'

'You're fifth on the list . . . should be about midday. Pop back on to your bed—we have to shave your leg and get you into a theatre gown.'

Despite his assumed nonchalance, it was obvious that he was beginning to get nervous. 'I *am* going to be able to play again after this, aren't I?' he queried.

Nicola and Karen exchanged mock-solemn looks.

'I wondered if he was ever going to touch the ball last time I saw him on the field,' said Karen, who was a soccer fan.

'Can only be an improvement then,' returned Nicola.

A slow grin spread over Gil's face. 'Watch it, you two, or I'll be chasing you round the ward, groggy knee or not! No, seriously, I mean, how long do you reckon it'll be before I can kick a ball again?'

'Do your exercises properly and you'll be out of here within a fortnight and you should have full movement within six weeks,' Nicola told him.

They shaved the leg and exchanged his pyjamas for a theatre gown.

'I'll be giving you your pre-med presently,' said Nicola. 'After that you won't know much about anything until you're back here again.' She checked that he had a name-tape on his other leg and wrist. 'Can't risk getting the wrong patient back, although anyone else might be an improvement on you.' She stepped adroitly out of his reach as he aimed a playful swipe at her.

There were three other cases for theatre. Sister Cromwell had given herself another half-day as she had to take her young daughter to the dentist. With patients needing to be monitored as they came round from anaesthetic, the remaining staff were kept on their toes. There were transfusions to be watched, pulses and blood pressures to be recorded and circulation in damaged limbs to be checked, in addition to the usual routine of the ward.

Gil Stevens surfaced at around three o'clock. His leg, now encased from ankle to groin in cotton wool and crêpe bandages over a back splint, was raised on a pillow to reduce swelling, while a cradle took the weight of the bedclothes. Although still drowsy, he was in considerable pain and Nicola was glad when Alex Baron arrived later, accompanied by Max, to check on their patients.

With Sophie talking on the telephone, it fell to Nicola to deal with the doctors. She had not seen the registrar since that first surprise meeting on the ward and in concentrating on her work she had forgotten the powerful impact of the man. Now, as the lusty, white-coated figure strode purposefully towards the nurses' station, her legs felt oddly weak.

'Any problems?' Alex Baron greeted her. 'With the patients, I mean,' he quipped, directing a meaningful glance at her from under his straight fair brows.

She ignored the veiled humour lurking in the depths of his keen eyes. 'Mr Stevens, the meniscectomy, is in quite a lot of pain,' she said.

'Right, we'll have a look at him.'

Max gave her a broad wink as they followed Alex Baron to Gil's bedside.

'Hallo, old chap. How are you feeling?' the registrar enquired, helping to draw the curtains round.

'Lousy, doc,' mumbled Gil.

Nicola turned back the bedclothes and removed the cradle so that the doctors could check on the leg.

'Circulation's fine,' remarked Alex, feeling the foot. 'OK, son, we'll give you a shot of something for the pain.' He took the clipboard and wrote up the medication. 'Nothing at all to worry about. It was a straightforward job . . . you'll be as right as rain in a few days.'

'Will you excuse me while I get this done?' said Nicola, taking the chart from him.

'By all means, Staff, if you feel it's urgent.'

'There's no point in people putting up with pain longer than they have to, is there?' she returned. 'It won't take a minute.'

She had the keys to the drug cupboard in her pocket. Together with Sophie she checked the pain-killer and recorded it in the dangerous drugs book, which they both signed.

'I'll give it,' Sophie offered. 'You'd better get back to His Lordship before he starts getting annoyed.'

The doctors were with Tom Woodman when Nicola rejoined them. 'Those stitches can come out now,' Alex confirmed, 'and we'll get another X-ray done tomorrow, to see if you can come down off this sling.'

Nicola smiled at Tom as she straightened the bedclothes and drew back the curtains before going on with the doctors to check on their two other theatre cases. They were both comfortable, having already received pain-relieving drugs.

Young Avril was watching her small portable television as they passed her four-bedded bay and Alex paused to talk to her. 'Your temp's been acting up, I hear. Why's that, too much excitement on the box?' She smiled shyly as he took her radial pulse beneath his strong fingers. He examined her leg wound through the window in the plaster. 'Yes, a bit of infection there. What did you put her on, Max?' he asked, turning to the houseman.

'Ampicillin,' said Max.

'Fine,' Alex nodded. 'Well, young lady, when are you going to start talking to us?'

She sighed and shrugged.

He patted her hand reassuringly. 'I'm sure there's nothing physically wrong. Your voice will come back in time. I'll get someone from ENT to check you over.'

He turned towards Nicola as they walked away from the bed. 'How's the courage these days?'

'Sorry?' she said.

'Managing to keep your tail up? Not meeting too many frightening females?'

Max looked mystified. He glanced from the registrar's satirical expression to Nicola's blushing cheeks. 'What goes on?'

'Just a private joke,' Alex explained.

'Oh, I thought she might have seen the ghost of Montfort Ward,' Max grinned.

'Ghost?' Nicola echoed. 'New hospitals don't have ghosts, do they?'

'Ah, but you see, this hospital was built on the site of the old priory,' said Max mischievously. 'Local legend has it there was this young nun who was walled up . . . she walks the ward at night searching for a way out.'

A shiver ran down Nicola's spine and she gave a nervous giggle.

'Now you've really got her worried,' smiled Alex, a fascinating hollow working in his lean cheeks.

She looked suitably disdainful. 'Is there anything more I can do for you? Because it's time I was off duty.'

They took their leave of her. She handed over the ward keys to Sophie and went off in the company of Meryl.

'Doing anything nice tonight?' Meryl asked her.

'No, nothing special. Are you?'

'I'm hibernating between now and the exam. I've simply got to get on with my revision.'

Nicola paused outside in the afternoon sunlight as they left the hospital building. 'Anything I can do to help?'

'We-ell,' said Meryl hesitantly, 'I've been going over the endocrine system . . . I suppose you wouldn't like to test me on it?'

'Sure, I'd love to. When, now?'

'Oh, that would be great. Come back to my room and I'll make us a coffee.'

'OK, just let me go and change first and then I'll be with you,' Nicola promised.

Meryl was in the students' hostel, a separate

building close by. The girls spent a profitable couple of hours together, with Nicola passing on the benefit of her greater experience on a number of points.

'Thanks ever so much, Nicky,' Meryl said when they at last called it a day. 'You've helped me more in one session than Dora Cromwell has the whole of the time I've been on her ward. She hardly ever does any real teaching.'

'Any time. Gosh! I'm starving, aren't you? Do they sell food at the Nun's Head?'

'Yes, they do quite a few things. Chicken-in-a-basket, mousaka, salads. Shall we go?'

As Max O'Malley had said, the pub was used by many of the hospital staff and Meryl introduced Nicola to a number of people. Having finished their meal at a table outside in the garden, they sat over their drinks enjoying the scent of roses in the border and listening to the evening bird-song.

'This is nice. I bet it's sweltering in London,' said Nicola. 'The pub we used to go to had its potted geraniums and some benches on the pavement, but that was about it.'

They were discussing the advantages and disadvantages of town and country life when Max came over to join them and the person with him had Nicola's eyes again popping in surprise.

'Neil!' she exclaimed, 'What are you doing here?'

'He's our ENT reg,' put in Max. 'You two know each other?'

Neil Chadwick grinned affably. 'Yes, we were together for a while at the Heathside. How come I've not caught up with you before, Nicky?'

'This is my first week here. I'm staffing on Montfort. Oh, it's great to see you, Neil,' she beamed, 'makes me feel quite at home.'

'Too bad I'm just about to move on,' he returned.

'Oh! Where are you going?'

'Coventry. But I'll be commuting until I find a flat there, so I'll still be around for a while.'

'And I thought you were complaining you didn't know anyone?' Max teased Nicola.

'I wasn't complaining, I just said.'

'How could you say such a thing with the enchanting Meryl for company!'

Meryl had been an interested bystander until then, but now when he turned his dark, twinkling eyes upon her, she flushed and laughed.

'He's been at the old Blarney stone again,' she said.

The look which passed between them left Nicola in no doubt that there was more to his teasing than blarney. They would make a nice couple, she mused. Max, a warm-hearted extrovert, and Meryl who liked mothering people. But what was she doing matchmaking with people she'd only just met! Even when you thought you knew people inside out, you discovered you didn't.

The conversation had turned to various goings-on at the hospital and to the life of the city. 'The place is riddled with history,' Neil said.

'I've always been a bit of a history addict,' Nicola returned. 'I shall have to go to the Tourist Bureau and pick up some literature.'

'You want to talk to Alex Baron,' suggested Max, 'he's the whizz kid on archaeology. Loves scratching about in the dirt and all that stuff. Did some on a London site when he was there, so I believe.'

'Oh?' said Nicola with polite interest. She privately decided she could manage quite well without Alex Baron's help. But it was a very pleasant evening and, back in her room when they had all parted company, she felt that her move to Priory Cross had been a good one after all.

On Saturday morning Nicola was up early to catch the train to London, looking forward to meeting her old friends. The train was quite crowded and she found a seat with difficulty, crammed between two sets of parents taking their children to London for the day.

Halfway through the journey, as before, an attendant came along to announce that refreshments were now being served. Her fellow travellers were already indulging in sandwiches and crisps and Nicola was not sorry to escape from the domestic scene for a while. Not having stopped for breakfast, she bought a ham roll to eat with her coffee and took it to a seat in the buffet car.

Someone jogged her elbow in passing as she raised her cup to drink. The person paused to apologise, and her startled eyes looked up into the lean, healthy face of Alex Baron. He was dressed with casual elegance in a fawn lightweight suit with the soft sheen of silk about his cream shirt.

'Hallo!' She felt peculiarly short of breath.

'Oh, no!' he exclaimed, 'Not skipping out on us already, are you?'

'Don't be stupid,' she returned, forgetting for the moment that she was speaking to the orthopaedic registrar. 'I have to go back to collect the rest of my things.'

'I see.' He parked himself on the seat opposite. 'May I?'

'Feel free.'

'The police have found my car . . . I'm going back to collect it,' he explained, emptying a sugar packet into his coffee and stirring.

'Oh, I am glad.' She was genuinely pleased for him. 'Was there any damage?'

'Not as far as I know.'

'And what about the papers and your luggage, are they intact?'

'They were in the boot, which should still be locked, so I'm keeping my fingers crossed on that one.' His dazzling blue eyes assessed her through the fringe of his thick lashes. 'Do you think you're going to like the Midlands, or will the lights of London entice you back before too long?'

'I'm not a quitter,' she retorted. 'Anyway, Priory Cross seems to have quite a lot to offer. As a matter of fact, I met someone I used to know in London, Neil Chadwick. That was nice.'

He raised his eyebrows with interest. 'The ENT chap? We're getting him to have a look at young Avril.'

'You don't seriously think there's any physical problem with her voice, do you?'

'No, but it doesn't do to take anything for granted. Question even the obvious, that's the best premise.'

'I hear we're to have the pleasure of nursing Sister Flint on Montfort soon,' she remarked, to keep the conversation flowing.

'Yes. Know her, do you?'

'We share the same kitchen in the nurses's home,' said Nicola with a wry smile, 'but that's about as far as it goes.'

His perceptive blue eyes glinted. 'I believe she has a reputation for being a holy terror. Will that worry you?'

She returned his gaze fearlessly. 'As far as I'm concerned she'll be a patient and I'll do my best for her, the same as I would for anyone.' They were nearing London. 'I'd better be getting back to my seat,' she said, finishing her coffee.

'I'll be driving back this evening. Can I give you a lift?'

'I shan't be coming back until tomorrow, thanks all the same.'

He rose when she did. 'Goodbye for now then.' And they parted company.

Back in her own compartment, Nicola sat in her corner absently watching the parents gathering their possessions together, putting toys in bags, wiping sticky faces and fingers and retying hair ribbons. Meanwhile, as the train rushed on towards St Pancras, her thoughts stayed with the man she had just left.

There was no doubt he sparked off some kind of reaction within her. Against her inclinations he attracted her, stirring feelings that she did not wish to encourage. When Leo died it was as though her heart had frozen. She shrank from any kind of involvement, even from confrontations with people. All she wanted to do was to lead a peaceful coexistence with the world.

Alex Baron had a point when he accused her of

timidity. Maybe she had become a complete and utter coward, but she didn't care. That was self-preservation. Yet the registrar seemed to be presenting her with some kind of challenge. Did he know, intuitively, that she had put the shutters up? *Get lost, Alex Baron!* she muttered to herself. *It's none of your business*.

Presently they drew in at the station. Nicola gathered up her weekend case, alighted and began walking quickly towards the exit. She was aware of the stalwart, blond-haired figure some yards behind her, but she hurried ahead not wanting to meet up with him again.

At the ticket barrier her heart sank as she recognised the searching, bold-eyed countenance of Simon Hill. His face brightened when he saw her.

'Hi, Nicky!' With easy familiarity he put his arms about her, kissing her full on the mouth.

She pulled away in time to see Alex Baron give them a sideways glance, striding past them. 'Simon!' she said, with a shaky laugh. 'How did you know I'd be on this train?'

'A little bird told me. Elaine thought you might like to be met, so here I am. You might look a bit more pleased to see me.'

'I'm surprised. I didn't expect anyone, that's all. There was no need.'

He took her weekend case, put his arm around her waist and walked her in the direction of his car. 'Well, I missed you, baby. Still liking it up there in the sticks?'

'Yes, it's fabulous. And what's more I don't have to keep fighting off wolves like you.'

He grinned and nuzzled his cheek against hers.

'Don't you realise the more you run, the more exciting the chase?'

Nicola let out an exaggerated breath. 'I wish you'd get it into your thick head that I'm not the slightest bit interested in being chased. You don't deserve Elaine. You're a shocker.'

'I know, but I'm lovely with it, aren't I?'

She hardly heard him. All she could think about was the derisive curl of Alex Baron's lips as he had caught her eye in passing.

CHAPTER THREE

NICOLA's return visit to London did not quite come up to expectations. To begin with, there was Simon embarrassing her with his unwanted show of affection in front of Alex Baron. Then, Simon's car had perversely refused to start. A good gynaecologist he might be, but he was certainly no mechanic. A couple of hours of her precious time were wasted while he fiddled about ineffectively before calling for a mechanic to come and sort out the trouble.

Simon was not the most sweet-tempered of men when things went wrong. 'Damn garages,' he growled, coming back from the phone. 'They can't promise how long they'll be, even though I said I was a doctor. If I keep patients waiting there's hell to pay.'

'Sorry, Simon,' said Nicola, feeling partly responsible for his plight.

'It's not your fault, my sweet. I wanted to see you. The trouble is I'm due at an outpatients' clinic at one, so I shan't have any time to be with you.' They sat in the car waiting. 'Oh well, better make the most of what time we've got. Tell me all your news.'

He put one arm around her shoulders and his other hand at a strategic place on her lap, moving it subtly. The warmth struck through her thin summer skirt and deliberately she moved the hand and

47

placed it back on the wheel. 'I thought you might have reformed. What a hope!' she said.

His fingers caressed the back of her neck beneath her long brown hair and he grinned provocatively. 'Come on, you know you can't resist me.'

Nicola sighed. 'I suppose it's wasting my breath telling you otherwise?'

'In my book *no* usually means *yes*.'

'Then I'll buy you a new dictionary,' she countered. 'How's Elaine?'

'Still totally committed to me, foolish girl. She should take her cue from you. Resistance makes the heart grow fonder.'

With relief Nicola spotted the arrival of a yellow breakdown van and pointed it out. 'Is that for us? Your "doctor" appeal must have done the trick.'

Their trouble proved to be nothing more serious than a loose electrical connection under the dashboard, and once diagnosed they were soon on their way.

'I bet you couldn't even change an electric light bulb,' Nicola joked.

'You're asking for trouble, young woman,' he retorted. 'As a matter of fact I'm rather good at feeling my way around in the dark. I'll give you a demonstration if you like.'

'I believe you. I don't need proof of that!'

Fortunately for Nicola there was only time for Simon to set her down at the flat before going on to the hospital. She rang the bell, but there was no answer, which presumably meant that Ros was at work as well as Elaine.

Searching under the broken tile in the small front

garden, Nicola found the key and let herself in. She made herself a drink before going to her old room to finish packing the remainder of her clothes in the large suitcase she had left behind.

On leaving the flat she had pushed the balance of her things to one end of the wardrobe, but it seemed strange to see someone else's skirts and dresses hanging where her own had belonged. In fact, she felt like an intruder messing around in a room which was not now hers. After filling the suitcase, she packed the remainder of her books and ornaments into a carton. That would have to be collected another time since she wouldn't be able to manage to take them both on this occasion.

Elaine came home and the girls greeted each other enthusiastically, exchanging mutual gossip.

'How's it going with Ros?' Nicola wanted to know.

'Oh, she's great. I say, nice of Simon to come and meet you, wasn't it? Did he tell you he knows a guy at your place?'

'Yes, someone in Radiology but I haven't met him. But then, I haven't met too many people so far. At Priory Cross everyone seems to know everyone else, except me. It's not like when you start training and you're all new together.' She related her first-night encounter with Sister Flint in the kitchen of the nurses' home. 'Believe me, *that* was an introduction! I felt like packing up and coming straight back.'

'Bet you did,' laughed Elaine. 'Still, it's the same when you go onto a new ward. At first you hate it, but you soon get used to it.'

'And another thing,' Nicola went on, I'd had this

argument with a guy I went up in the train with. He only turned out to be our orthopaedic registrar! I nearly fell through the floor when he appeared on the ward.'

Elaine looked curious. 'What were you arguing about?'

'I couldn't find my handkerchief—I'd been having a little weep after saying goodbye to you,' Nicola confessed. She smiled slowly, remembering, 'He told me to stop sniffing, blinking cheek. I yelled at him to get lost . . . and he took me for a cup of tea instead.'

'Good gracious, you *are* coming on,' said Elaine. 'I bet he was ninety.'

'No, he's thirtyish and quite impressive really. But a supercilious brute all the same. As a matter of fact I travelled back with him again today.'

'How come?' asked Elaine, her eyes widening.

'Oh, it wasn't pre-arranged or anything.' Nicola explained about the stolen car. 'Which was why I forgave him for being crochety the first time. But he keeps having digs at me about this and that. I've decided he's just another butch bully.'

Elaine glanced at her wrist-watch. 'I've got a hair appointment at three-thirty, but we've got time to eat out first.'

'OK, I'll come with you to the hairdresser's. I wouldn't mind having my own hair trimmed, if they can fit me in.'

Later that afternoon, on the spur of the moment, Nicola decided to have more than a trim and emerged from the salon with an urchin cut.

'Oh, I like it,' decided Elaine. 'It looks kind of elfin. Wish my hair were as manageable,' she sighed, running her fingers through her thick, wiry mop.

That evening there was a get-together of most of the old crowd at a local disco. There was the usual gossip about personalities and who was being seen with whom. But already new names were creeping in, names that were unfamiliar to Nicola, and she began to feel a little like an outsider.

Sunday was a pleasantly leisurely day and a crowd of them took a picnic on to the heath and finished up listening to music by the water until the midges began to bite.

To Nicola's relief Simon was not in evidence, being tied up at the hospital until after she left again for Leicester. This time her journey back was uneventful and she was less nostalgic than before. If her London visit had been vaguely disappointing, it had at least proved one thing. If you were going to make a clean break, then it should be a clean break. No use hankering after the old days. The past was past. At least with her new hairstyle she was returning with a new image.

The transformation did not go unremarked. Gil Stevens, the footballer, was quick to comment when she came to remove the pressure bandage over his knee on Monday morning.

'Hey, Nicky! What have you done to yourself?'

'Only had my hair cut. It's the new me!' she joked, carefully unwinding the cotton wool and crêpe bandages to take off the back splint.

'There was nowt wrong with the old one, far as I could see.' He inspected his still swollen knee joint. 'How d'you think that's looking?' he asked anxiously.

'Fine, Gil. But you'd better stay in bed until the doctors have been round. Can't risk you trying to put your weight on it yet. You have been doing your isometrics, haven't you?'

'Me *what*, love?'

'Contracting your quadriceps, wriggling your toes, etcetera!'

'Oh, sure. Old Arthur, the physio, makes certain of that.'

'Well, don't wait for him. Exercise as much as you can . . . both legs. The harder you work the sooner you'll be back on your feet.'

'I know.' Gil grinned. 'Then I'll be chasing you around, instead of vice versa.'

Meryl joined her to help bed-bath Tom Woodman. His pelvic sling had now been removed, also his catheter as his urine was clear of blood, but he still needed care in handling so as not to disturb the healing process.

'I'll be over there for a game o' draughts, matey, soon as they let me out o' this bed,' sang out Gil.

The two men had become good friends and it said much for Gil's cheeky optimism that the injured miner had become brighter.

Lunches were being served when Max O'Malley arrived with ENT registrar Neil Chadwick to make his observations on young Avril's voice problem. Sister Cromwell had gone for her own lunch-break, leaving Nicola in charge. She accompanied the doctors to the bedside, watching while Neil made his investigations and asked the relevant questions. Finally he was able to reassure Avril that all would be well in due time.

'It's not an uncommon happening,' he told her.

'Your vocal chords have gone on strike temporarily, but as you get better, so will they. You must make the effort to try and speak, but don't worry about it. That will only make matters worse.'

Leaving Avril looking happier, Max and Nicola saw Neil to the ward door.

'It's my farewell fling in the doctors' mess on Saturday. You will come, won't you?' Neil invited Nicola.

'Yes, I'd love to. I'm sorry you're going. It was nice meeting someone from the old days.'

'Oh well, as I said, I guess I'll still be in and out from time to time.'

'Drag Meryl along with you on Saturday, if she can tear herself away from her cramming,' Max suggested as they walked back to do the rest of the round.

'I'll try,' she said.

A number of patients had been discharged over the weekend and Monday afternoon was busy with admissions for tomorrow's theatre list. There were two elderly ladies for hip operations and another man for a meniscectomy.

Nicola did not have time to mention the invitation to Neil's farewell party until she went off duty with Meryl at four-thirty.

'Oh, I'd love to, but I can't!' Meryl sighed. 'The exam's next Monday and I haven't even touched the respiratory system yet.'

'Well, read it up tonight and I'll test you on it whenever we can fit it in. Go on, it'll do you good to let up for an evening. Max made a point of asking me to ask you to come,' she added.

'Did he?' Meryl showed more interest. 'OK then, maybe a break will do me good.'

Together they walked back towards the nurses' home and parted company. It was a warm summer's afternoon with the scent of blossom on the air. Back in her room Nicola washed and changed into easy clothes. She chose a cool, sleeveless pink T-shirt dress, discarded her tights altogether, and slipped bare feet into light strap sandals.

In search of company, she went across to Iris's room, but there was a note on the door saying Iris was on leave for a week. For want of something better to do Nicola decided to take herself into town for a meal.

The bus dropped her near the clock tower in the centre of the city. Most of the shops were closed and the traffic full of home-going workers. Nicola strolled down the High Street, looking in shop windows. A side street brought her to the picturesquely timbered old Guildhall, and she wished she had brought her camera. Late sunlight slanted through the trees lending a quiet peace to the scene—in spite of the traffic.

Further on there was an extremely ancient church with a squat, square tower and in front of that a large section of a carefully preserved old stone wall. She seemed to have stumbled across an important historical landmark. Stepping around to the excavated foundations on the other side of the wall, Nicola read the explanatory plaques which told her that these were the remains of the Roman occupation in the second century. Close by was a museum housing the archaeological finds, but that, disappointingly, was closed for the night. Oh well, some other time. There were obviously quite a few places to explore.

Beginning to feel hungry, Nicola turned back towards the city in search of a place to eat. She was hesitating as to the direction to take when a sleek, silvery-blue car pulled up a few yards ahead of her. The driver alighted and walked back towards her. And her pulse quickened at the sight of the long-limbed, bright-haired figure who approached.

'Hallo!' Alex Baron said, 'I thought it was you.' The deep, resonant voice sent a tingle down her spine. 'So you came back to us after all—albeit minus half your hair!'

She smiled a little uncertainly, running her fingers through her short cut. 'Yes, this is nice and cool for the summer.'

The sunshine-roof of his car was open and his own locks were tousled by the breeze. But he was immaculately dressed in a well-tailored grey suit and blue linen-weave shirt. It brought out the striking blue of his eyes, reminding her of the Aegean sea on her last holiday with Leo.

'What are you doing in this neck of the woods?' he said.

'Just mooching around, finding my bearings. I've been looking at the Jewry Wall. Fascinating, isn't it, to think of the Romans being here all those years ago.'

'Are you interested in archaeology?'

'Not passionately,' she admitted. 'Just generally curious about my surroundings. This is a new part of the world to me.'

The keen eyes meeting hers held a glimmer of amusement. 'I see. Well, if you've "done" this corner, can I save your legs and drop you off at your next port of call?'

'Oh, that's all right, thanks. I'm just going in search of a snack bar.'

'A snack bar?' He raised one eyebrow. 'That kind of diet won't fit you to battle with the Montfort Ward heavyweights. You'd better come and have a steak with me.' He propelled her towards the car, taking her agreement for granted.

'Is this the car you had stolen?' she asked.

He nodded. 'Yes. The only damage was a bit of paint off the rear wing. And the contents of the boot were all intact, I'm glad to say.'

'It must have been your lucky day.' She laughed at the wry look he gave her when she said it. 'I mean, it could've been smashed up.'

'Yes, maybe you're right,' he allowed.

Presently she was seated opposite him in a rather plush steak house, a lighted red lamp between them on the snowy tablecloth. Although slightly in awe of her host, she thoroughly enjoyed her meal. It occurred to her that she had indeed been existing on convenience foods for much of the past week.

He kept the conversation flowing by plying her with questions.

'So you've not been to the Midlands before. Where do you come from?'

'Essex, actually,' she said, taking a mouthful of the deliciously crisp side salad with her steak.

'You've given yourself a long way to go home, planting yourself up here.'

'Oh, my home's not there now. Well, it is, but it's let furnished for the time being.' She told him about her parents' move to America. 'They suggested I should go out there to work, but I haven't enough post-grad experience yet. Anyway, if I went out there, they might come back.'

'Problems, problems!' he said teasingly. 'And what are you passionately interested in, if not archaeology?'

'I'm interested in lots of things. But passionate is hardly the word.'

'Doesn't it even apply to the fellow who met you at St Pancras Station? His welcome seemed passionate enough.'

The remark embarrassed her. 'Call it what you like,' she said tersely.

'I just wondered if he was responsible for the previous tears? Kiss and make up, was it?'

'There *is* one thing I'm passionate about, and that's my privacy,' she retorted.

'Closed shop, eh?' He was not in the least put out by her annoyance. 'I admit I like to know what makes people tick. Part and parcel of my profession, I suppose.'

'Then you'll have to wait till I break a leg before you qualify for my confidences.' She suppressed a grin. It was impossible to be angry with him. And he had given her a slap-up meal. 'Don't wish it on me, will you? I'd rather not join Sister Flint on Montfort.'

'Mmmm!' He subjected her to a steady scrutiny. 'The idea has its attractions. If you were anchored in plaster of Paris, you wouldn't be able to run away. But I think Dora Cromwell would prefer you to be on your two feet.'

'I told you before, I'm not a quitter.' She was furious to find herself blushing.

'That's the spirit!' was his cheerfully patronising rejoinder. They finished their coffee. 'Now where can I drop you?'

'I'm going back to the nurses' home, but I'll get the bus.'

He would not hear of it, insisting that he was going that way in any case. It was ten o'clock when he set her down in the hospital grounds. About to enter the nurses' home, Nicola stopped to hold the door for Sister Flint, just coming off duty.

'Thank you. Was that Mr Baron's car I saw you get out of?' Sister Flint enquired with a touch of disapproval in her voice.

'Yes, he saw me waiting in town and gave me a lift back,' Nicola thought it best to explain. Hospitals were notorious hotbeds of gossip. She did not want tales to start circulating. Alex Baron might be married for all she knew.

The lift was waiting and Sister Flint grunted as they entered it. 'Oh yes, he had a meeting with Tresilian at the Infirmary, I believe.'

'Do you know yet when you're to come in?' asked Nicola, changing the subject.

'Thursday week, I hope, provided they can find me a replacement. Ever thought of doing an ITU course yourself?'

'Well, no. I think it needs a special kind of dedication to be able to cope with life and death situations all the time. I'd probably run out of hankies,' Nicola joked.

Sister Flint preened her feathers and even managed a wintry smile. 'I don't deny it's not everybody's cup of tea.' They arrived at the fourth floor and, with a dismissive nod, she hobbled on to her own room.

In a peculiar sort of way Nicola found herself looking forward to Tuesday and the prospect of seeing Alex Baron again, although his attitude irritated her. He had no call to treat her like a teenager, especially since he couldn't be that old, maybe just in his thirties.

She went on duty at midday and discovered Dora Cromwell in even more of a flap than usual.

'Mrs Rudkin's pin-and-plate has had to be post-poned till I don't know when. Would you mind going and telling her Nicky? We're getting an emergency straight from theatre, young chap with a partially severed hand . . . a sawmill accident. See to the bed, will you? You'll have to move that last hip replacement out of High Dependency.'

'Yes, Sister,' said Nicola. 'How long will he be?'

'Oh, not for some time. It's a big job so Alex said. Arteries, nerves and tendons to repair—everything, including bones.'

Nicola went to see Mrs Rudkin, who was waiting patiently in her bed for her turn to come. 'I'm ever so sorry about the delay, Mrs Rudkin, but the surgeons have had to fit in an accident case. A young man with a badly injured hand.'

'Oh! Oh dear,' said Mrs Rudkin, her old face wrinkling in sympathy. 'Poor lad. Well, I shall just have to wait then. Will I get done today, do you reckon?'

'Oh yes, I hope so,' Nicola smiled. 'Thanks for being so understanding.'

'Well, 'tis nobody's fault, love. And I'd want him

seen to if it was my boy, wouldn't I? Wish I could have a drink, though.'

'Sorry,' said Nicola, 'I know you must be dry. You can rinse your mouth out if you promise not to swallow any. I'll get someone to see to that for you.'

She asked Anna, a second-year student nurse, to take Mrs Rudkin a mouthwash and a bowl.

After that they pushed beds around to make a space in High Dependency and made certain that everything was in readiness to receive the casualty.

'Expect they'll want it in a Brooks' sling,' said Nicola.

'What's that?' Anna was new to orthopaedics, having recently transferred from a medical ward. An enthusiastic nineteen-year-old, she was keen to learn.

'We put the forearm upright in a roller towel suspended from an infusion stand. That keeps the hand elevated and reduces swelling. So we'll need two infusion stands, because he'll be having IV fluids. And put a vomit bowl, stethoscope and sphygmo on the locker, please Anna.' Nicola went off to check that Mrs Rudkin's X-rays were with her case notes.

It was five o'clock and Sister Cromwell had gone off duty when the phone call came that they could now give Mrs Rudkin her pre-med.

'You'll soon be on your way,' said Nicola, giving the necessary injection. 'We'll have to part you from your false teeth now, I'm afraid.'

Mrs Rudkin started to feel nervous. 'Oh dear, I've gone all wobbly. Th-that's the bit I hate about operations. I feel awful without my teeth . . .'

'Well, I'll see you get them in again just as soon

as you're round,' Nicola promised. 'Want to use a bedpan?'

'Yes, please.'

Anna came with a theatre gown and soon they had settled their patient down to get nice and sleepy before being wheeled to the theatre. By the time the porters arrived to collect her she was well sedated and tranquil, although glad of Anna's hand to hang on to as she was taken to the anaesthetics room.

Bill Platt, their new patient, was ready to be brought to the ward and Anna returned with him a few moments later. He was a large lad of eighteen with a round, country face and a shock of untidy brown hair.

'Mr Baron wants observations every fifteen minutes,' said Anna importantly, 'and this unit of blood's to run through by ten o'clock. He'll be up himself later. The boy's mum's here, by the way. She went to have a cup of tea, but she knows where to come.'

Nicola took over the transfusion pack and hung it up when the porters had transferred the youth to the bed. They arranged the covers over the semi-conscious patient.

'Now I can show you how the sling works, Anna.' Carefully placing the plastered forearm and hand in the suspended roller towel, Nicola secured it in an upright position. 'It's a comfortable arrangement,' she explained, 'and gives free movement of the shoulder.'

'It's his right hand, too,' observed Anna sympathetically. 'I bet he's right-handed. Do you want me to make out his charts?'

'Yes, please. Leave the case notes in the office. Then you'd better start the four-hourlies.' Nicola stayed to adjust the flow of the transfusion drip slightly, then she went in search of Karen and gave her the responsibility of specialling the boy. She was getting to know the staff now and knew that Karen was a girl to be relied upon.

In the office Nicola went through the case notes to find out the history of the accident and the extent of the damage. She had started to make out a sheet for the Kardex when an anxious-looking woman approached her. 'Excuse me, Nurse. They said my son was to be brought here, Billy Platt . . .' Her lips started to tremble.

'Oh yes, Mrs Platt,' said Nicola, rising from the desk. 'He's only just back from theatre and he's not properly with us yet, but you can come and see him.'

'How is he?' asked Mrs Platt, 'His hand—is it going to be all right?'

'Well, there was a lot of damage. Nerves and tendons and blood vessels to repair. I can't tell you a great deal as I haven't seen the doctors. They're still operating. But he's as well as can be expected at the moment.' She took the mother along to see her son and placed a chair for her by the bedside. 'You can stay with him for a while. He'll be very drowsy, but he'll probably be glad to know you're there later on.'

Mrs Rudkin was returned to the ward shortly after eight, having successfully weathered the repair to her femur which she had fractured in a fall. All being well she would be on her feet again within forty-eight hours. When she was fully awake Nicola returned her teeth, as promised.

Mrs Platt was still waiting in the hope of seeing the doctors, but her son had dropped off to sleep again after the injection of pethidine which had been ordered to relieve his pain. 'Would you like to wait in the day-room?' suggested Nicola. 'I'll get you a cup of tea.'

Alex Baron arrived with Max shortly afterwards. They went straight to Billy and the registrar inspected the fingertips of the damaged hand. 'So far so good,' he murmured. 'With a bit of luck we may have saved it. Had his pain-killer, has he?'

'Yes,' said Nicola. 'His mother's outside. She'd like to see you.'

He nodded and checked the transfusion. 'Call me at once if his blood pressure falls.'

Both doctors looked weary. 'Can I get you some coffee?' Nicola asked.

'I'm sure you've other things to do,' returned Alex with some impatience. 'Where's his mum?'

Nicola showed him to the day-room and left him. He was certainly right, she did have plenty to do. But it seemed like a brush-off, the way he had said it. As though he had regretted their socialising the previous evening, and she felt snubbed in consequence.

Max was in the office writing up case notes. 'Is that offer of coffee still open, Nicky?' he asked when she went in to start her report for the night staff.

'Yes, sure. I'll get you some. What's biting Baron?' she added.

'Oh, Tresilian was being his usual irascible self

today. Alex handles him better than most, but he leaves us all a bit frayed at the edges.'

'Oh!' said Nicola, who had yet to meet the volatile consultant. She went to the kitchen and made the drink before getting down to her writing.

'Thanks. Did you manage to persuade Meryl to come to the party on Saturday?' Max asked with studied casualness.

'Yes, I think she'll come.' Nicola could not help a private smile at Max's enquiry.

Finishing her report at last, she did a quick tour of the ward to make sure that all was in order before the handover. Night Staff Nurse Jean Arden, an SEN and a junior nurse had arrived and were in the office talking with Max when she returned.

'Well, I'm off too,' said Max, giving up his chair to leave the nurses to their briefing. He stretched and ran his fingers through his dark, curly hair, yawning. 'I'll just check on that boy before I go.' He looked in a few minutes later to remind them to collect more blood from the path lab.

It promised to be a busy night. One nurse went to start the late-night milk drinks while the other answered calls for bottles and bedpans.

Of the day staff only Nicola remained. 'Would you like me to get that blood for you?' she offered.

Jean smiled gratefully. 'Would you? That would be a help.'

Some twenty minutes later, having collected and delivered the blood, Nicola went off duty with a feeling of well-being. Crossing the gardens to the nurses' home, she caught sight of Alex Baron's car pulling away, and the memory of his snub when he had refused her offer of a drink dashed her spirits.

Was it because he'd had a tough time with Tresilian? she pondered. Or perhaps she'd only imagined the slight. Perhaps she was being over-sensitive about him, because of their strange first meeting. Anyway, she was glad that she had left the ward well-organised. Whatever the registrar's attitude towards her, she was going to give him no cause to find fault with her work.

One of the radiographers gave her a friendly smile in passing, which made her feel good again. How silly, she thought; someone smiles at you and it makes your day! Carving a niche for herself in the new environment was bound to take time, but already she was beginning to feel more at home.

It had been another hot day and even at ten p.m. the atmosphere was oppressive. It was a relief to strip off her uniform and take a cool shower before going to bed, covered in nothing but the sheet. Her windows were wide open, but no breeze came in. Sister Cromwell had given her another late duty the following day and the thought of not having to get up at six-thirty was welcome. She planned to have a long lie in.

Nicola read for a while before going to sleep, making a mental note to write to her folks the next day. At sunrise an enthusiastic dawn chorus roused her as effectively as an alarm clock.

'Shut up, you little perishers,' she muttered, turning over with her eyes determinedly closed, wishing she could remember what she had been dreaming about. But it was no use. The dream eluded her and so did sleep.

It was pointless just to lie there. Nicola went over to the window, leaned her elbows on the sill and her chin on her hands and watched the hospital world gradually awakening.

Not that hospitals ever slept. She remembered many lonely vigils she had kept with troubled patients in the small hours. And there was the endless tyranny of having to be watchful when your eyelids were drooping, and the sudden rush of vitality when faced with some two a.m. crisis. All through the night, life's little dramas continued to be played out in hospital. There were those who would never hear another dawn chorus and those who would be thankful to have got through another night. She wondered how the boy, Billy Platt, was this morning.

At twelve noon, dressed in a crisp, clean uniform, Nicola went over to the hospital canteen for lunch, finding Meryl there, also taking her lunch-break and moaning about Sister Cromwell having messed up the off-duty.

'I specially told her I had to have Monday for the Finals and she hadn't remembered. So you may be short-staffed.'

'You should worry!' Sophie chipped in.

'I expect we'll survive,' said Nicola. 'It's not theatre day. It should be fairly quiet.' She went on to tell Meryl about Max's further enquiry about the party. 'He must be keen on you,' she said.

Meryl grinned. 'It's taken him long enough to get round to it.'

That afternoon Nicola had her first introduction to the fearsome Mr Tresilian when he visited the ward with the rest of his team. She and Sophie were helping Mrs Rudkin back to bed after a brief sit out when the doctors descended upon them. Sophie rolled her big brown eyes and promptly made herself scarce. Sister Cromwell straightened her cap, put on her air of efficiency and summoned Nicola to bring the notes trolley and X-rays.

Mr Tresilian had an amazingly big voice for a small man, and fierce sandy eyebrows overhung his small slate-grey eyes. The team gathered around Billy Platt's bed.

'Well, young man,' boomed the consultant, inspecting the fingertips of the damaged hand, 'let's see you move those!'

Billy made a slight movement. 'I can't feel them,' he said, 'although it hurts like mad.'

'What d'you expect after trying to chop the whole thing off? You're lucky to have a hand at all.' Tresilian turned to Alex Baron. 'Give him plenty of pain control . . . he can go home as soon as you're satisfied with his general condition. I'll see him in outpatients in six weeks.'

Pig! Nicola thought, as she produced notes and X-rays, drew bed curtains and uncovered limbs.

Because of his skill the consultant commanded a certain reverence, but he was getting on in years and after all this time he should have acquired a little human understanding as well. True, with the ladies he was less forthright than with the men, although just as uncommunicative. Strange to say, he struck no terror into Nicola's heart. He just aroused her antagonism, and she was not at all surprised when he swept out of the ward without so much as a 'thank you' at the end of his tour.

Sister Cromwell's cheeks were pink with bother. She heaved a sigh of relief at his departure. 'That went rather well for a change,' she said. 'You kept a cool head, Nicky. Most people get fussed and produce the wrong X-rays or something.'

Nicola accepted the compliment with a smile. 'Horrid little man,' she said. 'However clever he is, it doesn't give him the right to demoralise people.'

'No, I agree with you. Thank goodness his kind are a dying breed. You wouldn't get Alex behaving like that,' said Dora Cromwell, 'and he's just as clever as the old man. In fact Tresilian takes the credit for a lot of the work that Alex does.' It was obvious she was the registrar's number one fan.

Alex came back to the ward a little later and had his own, more satisfactory, talks with the patients. Sister Cromwell was called to the telephone in the middle of his visit. He rejoined her in the office, where they were sitting in earnest conversation when Nicola went for her tea-break. They were still together when she got back.

'Something's come up. I have to go, Nicky,' said Dora Cromwell, 'but you'll be all right, won't you? Everything's under control.' She handed over the ward keys and gave a cursory report.

Alex Baron sat on, without comment, one long leg propped across the other. But all the while Nicola felt conscious of his eyes assessing her.

'OK, let's go,' he said, rising when Dora had finished speaking. 'Goodnight Nicola.'

The pair of them went off together. Nicola watched them go and saw Alex's arm slip about the sister's waist as they left the ward. With an effort she pushed the couple to the back of her mind and concentrated on the work to be done.

*   *   *

With a full complement of patients there was no list for Thursday and no more high spots of drama. Gil Stevens had his stitches removed and began to make progress with his walking, aided by Arthur, their resident physiotherapist. Old Mrs Rudkin also had been got up, but she was not yet confident enough to bear her weight on her leg. Avril was still lethargic, although her temperature had steadied.

All in all it had been an average sort of week as far as Nicola was concerned. She should have been content. Every day she was making new friends and finding her way about. But the picture that stayed in her mind was Alex Baron's arm protectively around Sister Cromwell. She knew that Dora had a daughter; she thought she had a husband. But if Alex and Dora were having an affair that was their concern and no reason for Nicola to feel disgruntled. All the same, she did.

CHAPTER FOUR

ON SATURDAY Nicola found herself quite looking forward to Neil's farewell party that evening. It would be a good opportunity of getting to know more people.

'What time do you think we should go tonight, Meryl?' she asked as they straightened Tom Woodman's bed before helping him back into it after lunch.'

'Nine-ish, I suppose. These things don't get warmed up until fairly late, do they?'

Sitting in a chair beside his own bed, Gil Stevens stopped exercising his leg muscles to ask where they were going.

'It's a farewell party for one of the doctors,' Nicola explained.

Tom looked anxious. 'Not Mr Baron, he's not leaving, is he?'

'No, Tom,' smiled Nicola, 'you're not going to have to get used to anyone new.'

'Wait till I get out of here,' Gil said, 'we have some good gigs at our club. You'll have to come. We can do with some new talent.'

'Why? Has someone muscled in on your territory since you've been out of circulation?' Meryl teased.

Gil gave a cheeky grin. 'I admit me style's been a bit cramped lately, but you wait till I'm back on form. I'll have 'em all lining up.'

'I don't know how they can stand the suspense!'

ribbed Nicola. 'I'm glad I'm not a football fan.'

He hobbled over and placed an arm around her waist. 'But you wouldn't have to join the queue, darlin',' he murmured, 'I'd let you in the back door.'

Laughingly she twisted out of his grasp. 'Push off, Gil. Once out of here and we won't see your heels for dust.'

'D'you wanna bet?'

'I never bet,' she returned. The smile was still on her face, but it left her eyes. Gambling was something she did not want to be reminded of. Was it always going to be like this? An innocent, casual remark by someone and Leo was there haunting her, filling her with futile regrets for the might-have-been. She shrugged off the mood, tidying back Tom's bed curtains in a brisk manner before they went on to their next patient.

With Sister Cromwell off for the weekend, ward routine on Montfort flowed smoothly and during visiting time Nicola was able to help Meryl with some more revision, as promised. They retired to an empty side ward and had an hour of uninterrupted study while Sophie Dakin and a student nurse manned the nurses' station.

The end of visiting signalled the resumption of work before both she and Meryl went off duty at four-thirty after arranging to meet up again at nine.

Back in the nurses' home Nicola had a bath and washed her hair. Her new short style had been well cut and her shining brown locks fell into place easily with a little help from her blow-dryer. Satisfied with the result, she was about to go along to the kitchen to make herself some toast when there was a tap on her door and Iris's fair head popped into view. 'Cooee, it's me!'

'Hi!' Nicola greeted her warmly. 'Come in! Did you have a nice holiday?'

'Super. It's been gorgeous in Scarborough. What's it been like here?'

'Sweltering. But it looks as if the weather's about to break soon, doesn't it?' Nicola said, glancing out of the window at gathering clouds.

'Oh well, the expectant mums won't mind it being cooler. Have you eaten yet?' Iris asked.

'No. I was just about to make myself something.'

'Come over to my room. My mum's packed me up with enough to feed the five thousand. I've got sausage rolls and fruit cake and strawberries out of the garden. I'll never get through it on my own.'

'Thanks. I'll go along and make the coffee then,' Nicola offered.

'No, come on, I've got my own electric kettle,' said Iris, leading the way. 'I hardly ever go to the kitchen. Can't stand sharing it with Flinty.'

It was the first time Nicola had been to Iris's room. Having had time to get properly established at Priory Cross, she had stamped her own personality on the rather stereotyped accommodation. There were bright posters on the walls, family photographs on her dressing-table, a small television and even a miniature fridge. Squatting on fat cushions on the floor the girls exchanged news and views while they ate, finding they had much in common.

'Well, I suppose I'd better be going,' said Nicola at last, glancing at her watch. She got up to rinse the coffee-mugs in Iris's wash-basin. 'Thanks for the grub. It's Neil Chadwick's farewell do in the mess tonight. Why don't you come?'

'Yes, might as well. I do know him,' said Iris.

'I'm meeting one of the girls from my ward at nine. See you later, then?'

Nicola went off to get herself ready. She decided on wearing a sea-green voile dress with thin shoulder straps. The colour made her limpid green eyes look even more striking and highlighted the creamy glow of her complexion. With pendant silver earrings, her hair fragrant and shiny, she felt in sparkling mood as she and Iris went down to meet Meryl in the entrance hall.

Five minutes' stroll brought them to the doctors' mess in the residents' quarters at the rear of the hospital. Lively music was underway when the girls arrived. A goodly number of people had already turned up and were standing chatting in groups.

Neil came forward to welcome them. With his tall, gangly frame and straight brown hair beginning to recede at the temples he had no claim to good looks, but his brown eyes were warm and friendly. 'So glad you could make it, girls,' he enthused. 'Come and have a drink.'

They went across with him in the direction of the bar and he stayed talking with them for a while when they were served. Meryl and Iris had a wide circle of acquaintances between them and were quickly at home amongst the cheerful gathering. Although they included Nicola it took an effort on her part to be bright and outgoing in this mainly unknown company. She felt a little shy and rather on the outside looking in.

Presently Neil came back to her accompanied by

a stocky young man with horn-rimmed spectacles, crinkly brown hair and a round, boyish face. 'Here's someone who wants to meet you, Nicola. Joe Lismore.'

Joe held out his hand and pumped hers vigorously, peering at her with a short-sighted smile. 'Simon Hill rang me recently and he mentioned you'd just joined us.'

Nicola smiled back at him. 'Oh yes, he told me he had a friend working here.'

'We-ell,' Joe hesitated, 'I'm not actually a friend, but we knew each other slightly in medical school. I was surprised to hear from him again. Wondered if he might be thinking of moving in this direction?'

'I don't think so. Actually he's my old flatmate's boyfriend. I suppose it just rang a bell when he heard I was coming here.'

'Ah,' said Joe, thoughtfully. 'I wondered what was behind it.'

Nicola had an inkling that Joe didn't rate Simon Hill too highly. Joe certainly did not seem the sophisticated Simon's type. He was too earnest and not over-confident.

'Would you like to dance?' he ventured after a while. 'I must warn you, I'm pretty hopeless.'

She laughed and put down her glass, going with him to the floor space where couples were dancing energetically. Joe's enthusiasm made up for his complete lack of rhythm and after a hilarious session Nicola felt thoroughly relaxed as they drifted back to the bar for a refresher.

People were arriving and departing all the time as their duties allowed. Nicola had lost contact with Iris and Meryl but she was enjoying herself in an unexciting sort of way. It was good to get to know people with whom she would sometimes be having dealings. Social contact often helped to oil the wheels on a professional level.

It was quite late before Alex Baron appeared on the scene. When she caught sight of him standing talking with Neil the evening took on an entirely different climate. Casually dressed in hip-hugging fawn trousers and a brown checked sports shirt, his body had the grace of a well-muscled big cat. It was ridiculous the way her inside flipped at the sight of him.

From then on what had been an averagely entertaining evening became an uncomfortable exercise in trying to avoid him. Making a determined effort to be a good mixer, she gave her full attention to the rest of the company.

Tongues loosened and reserves slackened as time wore on. Indulging in a smoochy dance with Neil, Nicola found herself wishing he were not leaving the hospital. He was a comfortable person to have around. Someone with whom you could have a mild flirtation and know that it meant nothing more than friendship. She caught sight of Max and Meryl looking dreamy-eyed together and glimpsed Iris having a vivacious exchange with one of the housemen and decided that the evening was satisfactory as far as they were concerned.

'Last orders, please,' sang out one of the medical students behind the bar.

'Anything more for you, Nicky?' Neil asked.

'No, thanks.'

'OK. See you later.'

She smiled as he left her and propped herself on

the corner of a table, feeling pleasantly sleepy. That was before she discovered that Neil had abandoned her in close proximity to Alex Baron. Then she could have wished herself anywhere but where she was. His back was to her on the other side of the small table. Nevertheless, a feeling of panic gripped her until, with relief, she heard Iris calling her name.

Quickly she turned her head in the direction of the voice—and it brought her nose in violent contact with a hard, blunt object. Tears sprang to her eyes.

'Oh dear, that was very silly of you, getting in the way of my elbow,' said Alex lightly.

She buried her face in her hands, not able to answer for the moment.

'Sorry, did I hurt you?' he said with a little more concern, removing her hands from her face and peering at her intently.

She gulped and groped for her bag on the table. 'I—I'll be all right in a minute.'

He pushed a handkerchief into her hands. 'Here you are.'

After wiping her eyes and tenderly blowing her nose, she blinked at him. 'Thank you.'

He eyed her askance, his mobile lips working to restrain a smile. 'This scene strikes a familiar note.'

'If someone hit *you* on the nose your eyes would water!' she snapped.

'True,' he agreed with irritating affability. 'Now, what can we do about it? Kiss it and make it better, as my dear mother used to say?'

Iris had come across, wanting to know what was the matter. Neil had also returned and was curious.

Alex explained. 'I've offered to kiss it better, but I don't think she fancies the idea.'

Putting the suggestion into practice, Neil kissed her lightly on the tip of the nose. 'There you are, doctor's orders.'

Nicola managed a watery grin. 'D'you mind? My nose has been assaulted enough already.'

Someone had put on a last slow record. 'Crisis over,' said Alex cheerfully and without any further preamble he whisked her into his arms, gathering her firmly against him as they moved to the music. 'A bit of excitement does wonders for the old adrenalin, doesn't it?' he went on. 'How are you facing up to life's other knotty problems these days?'

'What knotty problems?' she returned glibly, having recovered her equilibrium. 'There's nothing I can't handle.'

'I'm impressed.' There was a gleam of devilment in the eyes that looked down into hers. 'So you won't be planning another quick get-away to the south?'

'I may,' she said. 'I like to keep in touch with old friends.' At first she managed to meet his gaze squarely but the eye contact went on for too long and finally she blushed and looked away. This man was too virile and exciting. He sent ungovernable impulses surging through her veins, arousing feelings that she had no wish to be aroused—least of all with him. She knew precious little about him other than that he was a respected orthopaedic surgeon with an interest in archaeology. And an exalted opinion of himself, judging by his uppity attitude on occasions. He was definitely a man's man, but with his undeniable charisma he probably had women drooling over him by the fistful. Dora Cromwell amongst them.

Nicola's resolve strengthened to steer clear of Alex Baron. She could do without that kind of complication in her life. She stiffened deliberately. He relaxed his hold on her with a quizzically humorous lift of his straight brows.

'Thank you,' he said, with urbane politeness as the music ceased.

Afterwards a great many kisses were exchanged between a great many people, but Nicola took care to distance herself from Alex Baron.

People began to drift homewards. Someone came back for an umbrella and announced that it was pelting with rain.

'I shall have to make a dash for it,' said Nicola, making for the exit with Joe. 'I didn't bring a coat.'

'You'll get drowned,' he said, glancing from the downpour to Nicola's bare shoulders. 'Wait here a minute, I'll see if I can find you one of our white coats, that'll keep the worst off.'

She stayed in the vestibule while he went in search, but it was Alex who returned to find her. 'Joe sends his apologies. His bleeper went . . . he's wanted on the ward. And he couldn't find a coat.'

'Oh, not to worry. I'll just have to get wet.'

'No, you won't.' He pulled her back as she made to leave. 'My car's just round the corner. Stay here while I get it.'

'It's all right, don't bother,' she protested.

Alex commandeered Max who was about to dash off with Meryl under cover of an umbrella with a broken spike. 'Sit on this idiot-child for me while I get my car, will you? I can give you all a lift.'

Oh well, safety in numbers, Nicola decided, and she waited more at ease. And everything was fine when they piled into the silvery-blue car, except that on arriving at Meryl's hostel Max also left them to join her for a coffee.

Alex drove the remaining short distance with Nicola by his side. As they neard journey's end she grew more and more uptight at being left alone with this hunk of smouldering sensuality. Outside the nurses' home he braked and turned towards her, resting one arm along the back of her seat. 'Here you are,' he said. 'By the way, if you really are interested in the historical side of the city, I could show you around. I'm a native of these parts.'

The offer caught her by surprise. She didn't know quite what she had been expecting but it was certainly not that. 'Oh! Oh!' she repeated, hesitating, caught between inclination and self-defence. 'We-ell, I'm not sure of my off-duty. Y-you probably won't be free when I am . . .'

His mouth twisted into a wry smile. 'I was forgetting what a very private person you are. Well, there are some good official guides at the Tourist Bureau if that would suit you better—for the moment.' He leaned across, pausing before opening the car door for her. 'How's the nose now?'

'Fine, thanks.'

'Would you like a booster dose of my mother's remedy, just in case?'

Nicola's heart skipped a beat. 'I think I shall survive without it,' she murmured, reaching for the door handle.

His hand came down over hers. It was warm and magnetic, sending shock-waves through her. 'OK, we'll skip that one. But I missed out on the queue for your goodnight kiss. Wouldn't you like to put that right?' he queried coolly.

She passed her tongue over her dry lips as her heartbeat reached unbearable limits. 'No,' she said, swallowing.

His face was so close to hers there was scarcely a hair's breadth between them. She held her breath, feeling all the panic of a trapped animal.

With a mortifying chuckle he simply released the door catch. 'Go on, you'd better scram while you're safe.'

She did so, slipping out and running through the rain to the entrance without a backward glance. Once in the security of her room she sat on the bed with her head in her hands, her brain spinning. If he had been tender and persuasive instead of brittle and taunting she knew very well she could not have resisted him. For she had wanted to be loved, to feel again the sweetness of shared acceptance. And that was against all her protective instincts. Leo's memory was still too real. Love could also be slow torture. It was a chancy business. You could never be really sure of anyone, not completely.

An ominous rumble of thunder shook the air and the sound of the rain increased in intensity. Nicola got up to close her window as jagged lightning lit the dark sky. It seemed like an omen; elemental forces of nature over which she had no control. Sharply she drew her curtains across to shut out the storm. Weather was one thing, she told herself, but life was another matter. You were not a mindless creature at the mercy of fate. You made your own decisions and stuck by them.

Overnight the storm wore itself out, leaving plant life and buildings looking fresh and newly washed, the scent of the baptised earth rising with the warmth of the sun. It had been a quiet Sunday morning on the ward, Nicola learned, reporting for duty at midday.

Sister Cromwell seemed in excellent spirits as she gave her report before going off for her half-day. 'I'm glad the weather's cleared, we're taking my daughter to Warwick Castle this afternoon,' she confided.

'Oh, that sounds interesting. Does she like historic houses?' asked Nicola.

'Yes, history's her best subject,' Sister Cromwell put her reading glasses in her bag and handed over the ward keys before departing. 'It was always my worst.'

Nicola smiled. 'Who does she take after then, your husband?'

'Good Lord, no. The only thing he's interested in is sport. Actually, Alex Baron is taking us. He's Chrissie's godfather and she adores him. My husband and he were at school together.'

Nicola registered this casually-dropped information with mixed feelings. If there was a long-standing link between the two men, then why shouldn't Alex be close to Dora? She probably assumed a proprietary right to him in consequence, and there was no reason at all why Nicola should feel disgruntled.

Sister Cromwell went on. 'By the way, I've got my leave fixed up. I start on Wednesday. You're off tomorrow and Tuesday so I shan't see you again before then. Well, mustn't hang about or I shall get told off. Bye!' and she hurried away with her quick, tripping steps.

It was the first real conversation, apart from ward matters, that Nicola had had with her superior and she was glad to think that they might be getting on a friendly footing at last. She was nevertheless amused to discover that Karen's prediction had proved true. When Sister Flint came in to have her feet done Dora Cromwell would be conveniently absent.

Nicola started the drugs round with Karen and went on to give injections where required before making people comfortable for their visitors. She found Billy Platt attempting to fill in a crossword puzzle with his left hand. 'Good for you, Billy,' she said.

'Do you reckon I'll ever get back the proper use of my other hand?' he asked, his voice trembling ominously. 'There's still no feeling. I don't know what the doctors did exactly and I can't talk to that Tresilian bloke.'

She tried to be optimistic without raising false hopes. 'Well, I think they linked up all the nerves, Billy. As Mr Tresilian said, you're lucky they were able to save the hand. It may take some time, but I've heard of similar injuries doing well. Cheer up, you'll have physio once you get the plaster off, and you'll be amazed how things will improve with exercise.' She helped him change his pyjama jacket, rearranged his pillows and left him looking a little brighter.

Visitors began to drift in and Avril's mother

paused to speak to Nicola. 'I've got some good news for her at last, Nurse,' she said, her face glowing. 'Her boyfriend's come round. He woke up and spoke this morning, so his mum told me.'

'Oh, that's great,' said Nicola. 'Yes, that should buck her up. Did he have any other injuries?'

'No, just the concussion. They took an X-ray of his head but there was no fracture, so he was luckier than Avril. I don't suppose she'll believe it until he comes to see her. How long do they have to keep them in for that sort of thing?'

'They'll probably just want to keep an eye on him for a few days, all else being well.'

Mrs Jenkins heaved a sigh of relief. 'Perhaps Avril's voice will come back now.' She put a hand on Nicola's arm. 'Thank you all for being so kind to her, dear.'

'Avril's a nice patient, no bother at all, Mrs Jenkins,' smiled Nicola.

The weather continued fine. Iris was also off duty on Monday and the girls spent the day together, shopping in the morning and sunbathing in the afternoon. Later they made their way over to the staff swimming-pool which was being well patronised by people having a cooling splash after the heat of the day. Nicola was a good swimmer. Diving in from the deep end, she swam a fair way under water before surfacing. She waved to Iris sitting on the side dabbling her feet, her bikini still dry.

'You gave me a fright,' Iris called. 'I thought you'd sunk.'

Nicola laughed. 'Come on, get yourself in! I'm . . .'

The rest of her words were drowned out when a diver from the opposite side struck the water behind her, submerging her in a tidal wave. She spluttered and gasped for air. Then an arm locked around her waist and through her wet lashes she saw the face of Alex Baron. His eyes gleamed impishly.

'You really must try to keep out of my orbit if you value your skin,' he said, still holding her against his solid torso.

'Believe it or not, I'd really like to,' she flared. 'I suppose a simple apology is not in your vocabulary?'

'Apology? For what?' he demanded with wide-eyed innocence.

As he released her she vigorously splashed him back before streaking away towards the other end of the pool. With a few powerful strokes he overtook her, catching her by the legs and submerging her again. They surfaced together with their faces so close she could see the myriad blues that made up the striking brilliance of his eyes. She had expected the retaliation, but as they faced each other she could feel her heart thumping against his broad chest.

'You want to watch who you take on!' he warned.

'So do you!' she returned.

He gave the slow, twisted smile that she was coming to know. 'I'll try to remember that.'

Iris had at last got herself into the water and came to join them with a laboured breast stroke. 'You two larking about like a couple of dolphins, you make me feel like one of those bricks we used to dive for,' she puffed.

They each went their separate ways and presently the girls left the pool, put on towelling beach jackets and went back to tidy up before going over to the Nun's Head for supper. Meryl and a number of other third-year students were also there, holding an anxious post-mortem on the questions in the Finals exam which they had taken that day. Everyone thought they could have done better, everyone remembered things they should have included and didn't. Nicola and Iris exchanged smiles, remembering similar doubts and misgivings when they had been at the same critical stage.

'I'm glad that's all behind me,' said Nicola.

Iris wrinkled her nose. 'I've got another lot coming up next year. Anyway, after that I'm going to get some experience on a kibbutz. The world's my oyster!' she declared. 'How about joining me?'

Nicola smiled thoughtfully as they collected chicken salads and sat at a garden table to eat. 'I don't think that's me.' It surprised her to find Iris so adventurous. Frail-looking blonde she might be, but she certainly knew where she was going.

The midges were beginning to be troublesome and after waging an unsuccessful battle with them, the girls were driven inside to join the others. Going to the bar to collect more drinks, Nicola's heart sank to find Simon Hill standing there having a beer with Joe.

'Hallo, beautiful,' he greeted her, enjoying her surprise.

'Hallo!' Where did you spring from?' she said, disconcerted.

'I was in Birmingham for a symposium yesterday so I decided to look up Joe. Spent last night at his place. We've been trying to pin you down all day. Where've you been?'

'Day off,' Nicola explained, glad that she hadn't been available. She ordered her drinks.

'I'll get these,' said Joe and they accompanied her back to where she had left Iris. Nicola made the introductions.

'When do you go back?' she asked Simon.

'Tonight, more's the pity. By the way, Elaine asked me to drop in some more of your gear while I was here. I left it at Joe's actually. What say you and I slip out there now and get it?'

'Well, I—er,' Nicola hesitated, 'perhaps Joe wouldn't mind bringing it over for me sometime?'

'Oh, we don't want to bother Joe, do we?' breezed Simon. 'Anyway, he's on call. It won't take us long.'

There seemed no option. Much against her inclinations Nicola took her leave of the others and set off in Simon's car towards Joe's flat.

'That's got rid of them,' he declared with satisfaction as they drove off into the darkening countryside. 'I deserve some time alone with you after all my trouble, don't I?'

'It was nice of you, Simon,' Nicola agreed reluctantly, 'but there was no need for you to bother about my bits and pieces.'

He cast her a sideways grin. 'That's where you're wrong. I'm very concerned with your bits and pieces.'

She made a face at his innuendo. 'What was your symposium about?'

'Oh, there's always some joker with new ideas on childbirth. So long as no one finds a way to transfer gestation to the father, I'm happy.'

Fifteen minutes drive brought them to an area of impressive old red-brick mansions in well-established gardens. Simon pulled up outside one of them.

'This is an affluent sort of neighbourhood,' she remarked.

'Apparently the hospital owns a number of these places and lets them out in flats to the medical staff. Coming in?'

'No, I'll wait here.'

'Oh, come on, love. Joe won't mind.'

'There's no point, Simon. You've only got to pick up the stuff.'

'We might try the bed for size,' he returned softly, running a finger slowly down the back of her neck. 'Admittedly it's only a single, but space is relatively unimportant.'

She gave an exaggerated sigh. 'Would you believe that I came up here deliberately to get away from you?'

He looked knowing, continuing to stroke the back of her neck. 'So what are you doing here with me now?'

'Oh, cut it out, Simon! I'm not coming in with you.'

'Well, it's much easier in bed, but if you prefer it this way . . .' Deliberately he leaned towards her, clamping his mouth over hers, forcing her head back against the seat.

She squeaked and tried to wriggle free. 'No, Simon, no!' she protested, twisting her face away.

'Oh yes, Nicky, yes!' he persisted, his lips travelling to her throat, his breath hot on her skin.

'I shall get really mad with you if you don't stop it.'

'And what are you like when you're really mad?' he murmured provocatively, looking into her face while his hand teased her breast.

Angrily she thrust the hand away. 'I'm not playing. If you don't behave yourself, I'll . . .'

'You'll what?' His voice was husky, urgent. His hand, inching up her skirt, stroked the soft silk of her thigh. She could see the glitter in his dark eyes and realised with frightening clarity that she was no match for his physical strength if he insisted on having his way. His breath was coming quickly. She stiffened as he positioned himself to manoeuvre a leg between hers. Then, instinctively, she kneed him hard in the groin.

He groaned and fell back into his seat clutching himself. 'You bitch!' he gasped.

Nicola grabbed her chance. She slipped out of the car and ran. She had no idea where to. Rounding a corner she ran full pelt into someone. Her bag fell to the pavement, its contents scattering.

'Sorry,' she panted as strong arms caught her.

'And what are you running from this time?' asked a deeply curious voice.

Looking up she was dismayed to find her way blocked by Alex Baron.

CHAPTER FIVE

'SORRY,' Nicola said again in a breathless voice. She stooped to pick up the contents of her bag and Alex bent to help her, quietly handing her back lipstick, comb and purse.

'Well?' His keen eyes scanned her troubled face. 'What goes on?'

'N-nothing. I—I'm trying to find a bus,' she said lamely. Her bottom lip would not stop quivering and she caught it between her teeth.

'You're a long way from buses. The last one's probably gone, anyway. And what are you doing, running around here on your own?'

'I wasn't on my own to begin with,' she shrugged. 'I just decided I didn't want to stay on at this—er—party.'

His eyebrows lifted fractionally. 'Whoever's party it was might have had some regard for how you would get back. *Now* what are you going to do?'

The sound of a car made her glance over her shoulder. But it wasn't Simon's flashy scarlet Triumph and it sped on by. Her limbs were shaking. 'D-do you live near? Could you get me a taxi?' she ventured.

He put his hands on her shoulders and turned her about. 'Come on, you'd better come back to my place for a moment.'

Walking her a short distance, he lead her into the

driveway of a mature, detached family house. It was built of the good red brick typical of the area. Banked hydrangeas flowered beneath the square-bayed windows. The heavy white-painted front door in which he inserted his key had a circular stained-glass inset.

'It's all right,' he said, ushering her through into a square oak-panelled hall. 'There's no one here but me. Go and sit down in there. I'll make you a coffee.'

She went into the room he indicated and perched on the edge of a deep-cushioned, chintzy sofa. Smoothing her dishevelled hair and straightening her cotton skirt, she took long, slow breaths to calm herself and had found some composure by the time he returned.

Setting two mugs of coffee on a low table near her, he lowered himself into an easy chair and crossed his long legs comfortably. 'Sit back and relax. You don't have to be prepared for immediate take-off, you know.' Square chin propped thoughtfully on his fist, his eyes narrowed as he watched her.

She eased herself back onto the seat, concentrating her gaze on the York stone fireplace, its grate filled with dry logs, then her eyes wandered to the bowl of garden roses on the sideboard. Anything to avoid his perceptive scrutiny.

'Well, who was it?' he rapped out in a voice that made her jump. 'That guy at the ticket barrier?'

Round-eyed, she darted him an uncertain glance.

He smiled wryly as she neither confirmed nor denied his shot in the dark. 'My dear girl, I don't go around with my eyes shut. I know he was at the hospital today. He had lunch in the mess with Joe Lismore. I guessed it wasn't only Joe who brought him here.'

She flushed, picked up her coffee and sipped it without answering.

'You won't want my advice,' he went on crisply, 'but I'll give it to you all the same. Someone who makes you so unhappy is not worth wasting your time over.'

Nicola managed a light laugh. 'You've got it all wrong,' she said, but she didn't enlighten him.

For some reason Alex seemed short of temper, certainly not in the playful mood of their encounter in the pool that afternoon. His laser eyes seared into hers. 'I may have got something wrong, but not everything,' he said. 'However, I'm prepared to leave it at that for the time being.'

There was an odd, melting sensation in her bones. Strange how one brooding glance from this man could have such a disturbing effect when all Simon's sexual advances left her with nothing but distaste.

'Do you share this house with anyone?' she asked, irrelevantly.

'No. This one doesn't belong to the hospital. It's my old family home. My parents are both gone now, but I keep it on for sentimental reasons. That, and being too lazy to move. Anyway, it's convenient in lots of ways.'

His bleeper sounded at that point and with an exclamation of annoyance he leapt up and crossed to the telephone.

'So much for my planned quiet night,' he said

after a brief exchange, 'There's been a pile-up on the M1—I shall have to hurry you.'

'Yes, of course.' Quickly she downed the rest of her drink.

'Are you back on duty tomorrow?' he asked as they drove back in the direction of the hospital.

'No, not until Wednesday afternoon.'

'Dora's on leave then,' he said, half to himself.

'Yes. Did you enjoy your visit to Warwick Castle on Sunday?'

His lips twitched with amusement. 'You're very well informed.'

'Sister Cromwell just happened to mention it.'

'I see. Yes, it's a fascinating place. But wherever you go the company makes all the difference, doesn't it?'

Nicola nodded. On second thoughts she was sorry she had mentioned it. She didn't want him to get the impression she was the slightest bit interested in his doings outside the hospital.

'You must let me know if you'd like to see the place yourself,' he said casually. 'Perhaps we can arrange something.'

'Thank you.' Nicola was equally casual. 'I'll bear that in mind.'

It was midnight when they parted outside the Accident and Emergency department. 'I hope they don't keep you up too long,' she said.

'What you might call the end of an action-packed day. Bye. I'll try not to fill all your beds.'

Nicola went across to her room counting herself lucky. At least she had an undisturbed night ahead of her. He faced the grim task of helping to piece together broken bodies, possibly having to break bad news to distraught relatives.

In the corridor she met Iris coming from the bathroom. With her mind a maelstrom of conflicting emotions Nicola was not in the mood to talk but Iris was as voluble as ever.

'Hi! Did you have a nice evening with your friend?' she asked brightly.

'Simon? Oh, he's a bit of a pain really. Just someone I used to know in London.'

Iris laughed. 'I got the impression Joe wasn't too keen on him either. We were getting on famously,' she confided, 'but Joe didn't like to go back to his place for fear of butting in on you two. I'd just about got him poised for passion when he got bleeped for A and E and had to go.'

'Shame,' said Nicola. 'That's what you have to expect if you get involved with doctors.'

'Mmmm . . . better to opt for someone with a nine-to-five job, like a bank, wouldn't it?'

Would it? If only you knew, thought Nicola, Leo's image appearing before her eyes.

'Has Simon gone back now?' Iris went on.

'I haven't the foggiest. I left him at Joe's, actually. Alex Baron had to come in for the crash— he lives near Joe—so he brought me back.'

'Did he? What have you got that the rest of us haven't? He's the most elusive bachelor in the business.'

Nicola smothered a yawn. 'He can stay elusive for all I care. I'm not interested in him, or he in me. Tonight was just a matter of convenience.'

'What about that mating display in the pool earlier on?'

'Mating display?' Nicola giggled. 'That was merely a show of male supremacy when I dared to splash him back after he'd deliberately drowned me, the wretch. I bet that shook him.' She struck a dramatic pose and recited, 'I know I have the body of a weak and feeble woman . . . but I can give as good as I get, as Mr Alex Baron will find out!'

Iris's laughter tinkled down the corridor.

'Shh!' warned Nicola putting a finger to her lips. 'You'll have Sister Flint waking up. Oh gosh! That reminds me, she's due in this week for her bunions. Pray for us, won't you?'

They parted company and Nicola had a cursory wash in her room before flopping into bed. Tired though she was, she could not get Alex out of her thoughts. In her mind's eye she saw him sitting opposite her in his living room, awesomely stern, not attempting to conceal his hostility when he had spoken about Simon. His impact on her was bewildering. He was both chilling and inflaming. She wanted to run a mile and yet he attracted her. There was an aura about him, like the warmth of the sun, undeniable in its allure, yet dangerous if abused.

Had he really been concerned for her, or would he have given the same advice to any girl who seemed to be in a mess? There had been that bowl of roses in his living room. Men on their own did not usually bother with flowers. He'd said the house was convenient for lots of reasons. Perhaps Dora Cromwell was one of them. Maybe she'd put the flowers there. Maybe she had gone back there after Warwick Castle?

Oh, for goodness sake! Alex was a man of the

world, and an attractive one. Because he was a bachelor it didn't mean he had to be a saint. Men took what they wanted where they could get it. All the same, unlike Simon, he had made no attempt to make a pass at *her*. So what? Perhaps she just didn't appeal to him. Anyway, where romance was concerned she was a disaster area: best to give it a wide berth.

On Wednesday morning before going to her ward Nicola went along to the X-ray department and sought out Joe, catching him between patients. She felt she should apologise for landing him with the things that Simon had brought up for her.

'Sorry about the other night, Joe,' she said. 'Simon and I had a bit of a tiff. He decided to go straight back to London.'

'Yes, he left me a note to say he was pushing off.'

'The thing is, I didn't get to pick up my gear so it must still be at your place.'

Joe frowned and pushed his glasses up on his nose to peer at her. 'I don't know of anything, Nicky.'

'Oh well, perhaps he took it back again with him,' she said with a shrug, deciding that might be the sort of thing Simon would do out of pique.

'If I come across any strange property I'll let you know,' Joe promised.

On the ward Nicola found Jean Arden in charge. Jean, newly off nights, was a tall, slim, unhurried girl with a placid temperament. She met every kind of situation with aplomb, which made her a good person to work with.

Jean briefed Nicola on the state of the ward. 'Gil Stevens went home this morning—he said he was sorry not to say goodbye to you. Billy Platt also went home, and old Mrs Yelverton. There's a Mr Geoff Naylor in with Tom Woodman now. He came in on Monday, prolapsed intervertebral disc. He's had a myelogram. He's got some neurological symptoms, diminished sensation in feet and legs and a bit of tingling. They've decided to inject the disc this afternoon. I haven't laid up the trolley yet, by the way.'

'OK,' said Nicola, 'I'll do that. Who else is on?'

'You've got Karen and Anna, and Sophie'll be back from lunch in a moment.'

'Has Sister Flint booked in?'

'Yes, she's in the side ward. We've done her obs,' Jean yawned languidly. 'My wretched time-clock hasn't caught on yet . . . it takes me ages to adjust from nights to days. Well, I'll go to lunch then,' she said as Sophie returned. 'Anna asked to see that trolley laid up, if you wouldn't mind.'

Nicola quickly flipped through the Kardex to remind herself of the patients' treatments before going to find Anna and show her how to prepare things for the lumbar puncture.

'It's a strictly aseptic technique,' she explained, 'but everything comes in sterile packs. Wipe the trolley down with Dispray first, then put all the equipment on the lower shelf.' In the store-room she detailed and selected the items required, letting Anna do the placing. 'We'll need a sterile gown, mask and gloves for the doctor. Put a sterile cloth on the top shelf, and there you are. It'll be done in the treatment room so we'll wheel his bed down when the doctor arrives.'

'Oh, thanks,' said Anna enthusiastically. 'That's great.'

'Now if you'll bring a theatre gown we may as well get Mr Naylor ready.' Nicola went off to introduce herself to the new patient. She found a tall, thin man in early middle age, lying flat with one pillow, his lean face anxious. She smiled at him warmly. 'Hallo, Mr Naylor. We're just going to get you ready for your lumbar puncture. Is this the first time you've slipped a disc?'

'Yes, Nurse. I was lifting a bag of cement when it happened. So much for do-it-yourself!'

She drew the curtains around his bed as Anna arrived with the gown.

'Will it be painful?' he asked apprehensively.

'You'll have a local anaesthetic first, so it shouldn't hurt,' Nicola reassured him as they exchanged his pyjama jacket for the gown.

'Do you think I'll need an operation?'

'Traction and rest will often do the trick, so don't worry about operations just yet.'

'It's a question of how long I can afford to be off work.' His forehead wrinkled. 'I've got a wife and three kids to think about.'

'Well, let's see what the outcome of the investigations is first, then we can get our medical social worker to have a chat with you,' said Nicola encouragingly. 'You might be entitled to some extra social security benefit.' They pulled back his bed curtains and left him talking to Tom.

'You start the TPR's, Anna. I'd better go and say hallo to Sister Flint.' Nicola hurried down the ward and went into the side room with a welcoming smile. She found Sister Flint sitting by her bed reading. She was wearing a newish turquoise nylon dressing-gown, the frilled lace at the neck of her warm pink nightie looking oddly out of place with her poker face and cropped, iron-grey hair.

'Good afternoon, Sister,' said Nicola cheerfully. 'Everything all right?'

'Oh, it's you, is it?' Sister Flint's set features relaxed a little. 'Yes, except that you might take my lunch tray away. The ward maid seems to have forgotten me.'

'Oh dear, haven't you had your cup of tea yet?'

'No. Out of sight, out of mind.'

'I'll get you one now. You should have rung your bell.'

Sister Flint sniffed. 'Mustn't start off by being a nuisance. Have you got the theatre list yet? Do you know what time I'm down for?'

'It's in the office. I'll check and let you know.' Nicola gathered up the tray of dirty dishes and went to the kitchen to have a word with Millie, the ward-maid. 'Don't forget Sister Flint in the side ward . . . she hasn't had any tea.'

'Oh, my Gawd,' said Millie, putting a hand to her mouth.

'Make her a fresh one, will you, and I'll take it in.'

Having checked the operating list Nicola took in the tea. 'They're not keeping you hanging about, Sister, you're down for nine a.m. tomorrow.'

There was a tap on the door and Mrs Young, the Senior Nursing Officer, looked in. 'Am I interrupting anything?' she enquired.

'No, come in.' Nicola brought forward a chair. 'Would you like some tea?'

Mrs Young shook her head. 'I've just had some, my dear. Anything I can do for you, Hilda?'

Excusing herself to get on with her work, Nicola left them talking. Outside she caught up with Mrs Rudkin, on crutches, making her careful way back from the bathroom. 'My goodness, you've made progress since I was last on. You're almost ready to take part in a marathon.'

The patient chuckled. 'I think I'll be taking it steady from now on, but I'm not doing too badly, am I? Going home to my daughter's at the weekend.'

'Good, I'm glad you've got someone to look after you.'

'Yes, she's a good girl. Here she comes now.' Mrs Rudkin nodded towards the door where the first visitors were arriving. Following her gaze Nicola also saw Alex and her pulse quickened as she went to join him.

In the office he studied Mr Naylor's case notes. 'Did you manage to keep out of mischief yesterday?' he murmured without looking up.

Her colour heightened. 'Coming from you that's a cool thing to say.'

He eyed her intently. 'Why coming from me? I thought I came to your rescue rather nobly the other night?'

His involvement with Sister Cromwell had been uppermost in her mind but she realised she had spoken out of turn. 'You've come to do the lumbar puncture, I suppose?' she said as levelly as possible.

'Yes, are you going to help me?'

'If you'd like me to.'

'There's no one I should like better. Are we ready?'

'Yes, I'll get him to the treatment room.'

With the aid of an auxiliary nurse she wheeled Mr Naylor in his bed to the treatment room where Alex was already stripping off his white coat. 'Hallo, Mr Naylor, nothing to worry about,' he assured the patient, 'and having Nurse Pascall to hold your hand will more than compensate for any slight discomfort,' he joked.

Nicola rolled her eyes heavenwards and the patient managed a laugh. She produced face masks for herself and the doctor. He scrubbed his hands and put on his sterile gown, turning so that she could tie the tapes at the back. Then she opened the sterile glove pack and held it out to him. For the next few moments they were both too concerned with the matter in hand for further banter.

Nicola supported Mr Naylor on his side while the registrar decided on the exact point of entry for the puncture after injecting the local anaesthetic. 'All right, sir?' he enquired. The patient nodded. 'Now I'm going to extract a little of your spinal fluid,' Alex explained as he worked, 'and then I shall put an anti-inflamatory drug into the disc.' He studied the small manometer attached to the syringe and murmured, 'Mmm . . . pressure's OK.' When the process was completed he gently withdrew the needle. 'There, that's all there is to it. We hope that will improve matters.'

He nodded towards Nicola who placed a small sterile dressing over the puncture wound. 'Carefully on to your back again now, Mr Naylor.' She took a gauze swab from the trolley and wiped the beads of perspiration from his face. 'Just you lie quietly like that for a while. Let me know if you get a headache and we'll give you something for it.'

Mr Naylor was returned to his cubicle and Nicola cleaned up the equipment before going to the office to record details of the process on the Kardex. Alex was still there, busily writing. 'We make a pretty good team, don't you think?' he remarked.

'I haven't had any complaints so far.'

'Not even from Sister Flint?'

'Not even from Sister Flint.'

He raised his blond head to look at her, his mouth working to restrain a smile. 'Tresilian and she have this on-going battle. Have had for years apparently, so look out for fireworks.'

'He ought to have more sense than to upset her when she's vulnerable,' retorted Nicola, 'but on the whole men are rather short on sense, I find.'

'There speaks the voice of sad experience. Never mind, one day you'll find him.'

'Who?'

'The man with sense enough to put a noose around your little neck and lead you up the aisle.'

She flung him a mutinous glare. 'Will you kindly go away if you've finished what you're doing? Some of us have work to do.'

'Yes ma'am!' He rose to his feet and saluted smartly. Then he dropped an arm around her shoulders, whispering, 'Perhaps I'll take up rope-throwing myself. Now there's a thought.'

Angrily she shook him off and he laughed as he left. 'Just popping in to see Hilda to get her to sign the consent form.'

Her eyes followed him, seeing him breeze into the side ward with a devastating smile. No doubt he would have Sister Flint eating out of his hands. That smouldering charm of his could melt an entire glacier. Thanks goodness her own defences were alert and working well. She was never going to lay herself open to heartache again.

The rest of the day passed busily after visitors left and by nine-thirty Nicola was glad to hand over to the night staff. Before going off duty she went to say goodnight to Sister Flint. 'I'm not on until midday tomorrow, so when I see you again it will all be over, won't it?'

'Who's going to be on?' demanded Sister Flint, looking disgruntled.

'Jean Arden will be here.'

'Oh, that's all right then. Goodnight.'

Back in the nurses' home Nicola telephoned Elaine to find out if Simon had indeed taken her belongings back to London again.

Elaine sounded completely mystified. 'What are you talking about?'

'The remainder of my stuff that you gave Simon to bring up for me.'

'I didn't give him anything to bring up. It's all still here. I didn't even know he was going to be in Leicester. He was supposed to be going to Birmingham.'

So that was it. Simon had lied. It was just a fabrication to get her away from the others. She might have guessed as much! 'Well, he did go to Birmingham, but he popped in to see Joe Lismore, that friend of his, on the way back,' said Nicola. She hadn't the heart to disillusion her friend. 'Perhaps we got our wires crossed . . . I only saw him for a few minutes.'

'I'm pretty fed up with him, I can tell you,' Elaine moaned. 'He's been in a foul temper ever since he got back. I feel like telling him to get stuffed.'

Nicola had heard her say that before but it was only an idle threat. 'He's always been a bit explosive, hasn't he? Let's face it Elly, he wouldn't be the easiest bloke to land yourself with.'

'I've been having a thin time all round since you left,' sighed Elaine. 'Ros is OK as a person, we get on fine, but the flat is a tip. I seem to spend all my time tidying up after her.'

'Like that, is it? Look, why don't you come up here on your next days off? Let me know when and I'll fix mine for the same time.'

Leaving Elaine sounding more cheerful, Nicola went to see if Iris was in and found her sprawled on her bed eating potato crisps and watching TV.

'Hi!' Iris jumped up and turned off the programme. 'I've got some news for you. Want a coffee?' She filled her kettle and got out two mugs.

'What news?' Nicola kicked off her shoes and perched cross-legged on the end of the bed.

'I went to that meeting tonight . . . about the summer fête the Friends are putting on. The social sec was asking for ideas and a girl from your ward—Jean Arden—suggested a kissing booth. They'd done it at her previous place. Well, to cut a long story short, we put your name down for that. I was sure you wouldn't mind.'

'A *kissing* booth?' squeaked Nicola. 'Thanks very much! Exactly what have you let me in for?'

Iris giggled. 'We charge twenty pence or something for a kiss. Customers can choose their own type. Jean is calling herself Legs Eleven—her legs go up to her armpits, don't they? I'm going to be the Blonde Bombshell and you can be Pocket Venus. Should be a laugh, shouldn't it?' She handed Nicola her coffee. 'We only have to do it for about an hour, then three others take our places.'

'I wonder how many people you can kiss in an hour?' mused Nicola.

'I shall charge extra if anyone hogs it. Hey, I delivered my first twins today,' Iris prattled on, 'and the father kissed me before he kissed his wife. She didn't seem to mind though. How are you lot getting on with Sister Flint?'

'Oh, she's all right. Fairly docile, really. Expect she's got a few butterflies, the same as anyone before an operation. Alex Baron was in there this afternoon turning on the charm. That'll probably keep her sweet unless someone does anything absolutely stupid. I'm on another late tomorrow and she's book for nine so I shan't have the privilege of prepping her, thank goodness.'

'Joe and his flatmates are planning a party soon,' said Iris. 'One of them's moving on. I think it's to be after the fête, but I'll let you know.'

Nicola took herself off for a bath and bed. She was glad she had made the decision to come to Priory Cross. Most of the people were friendly and her social contacts were growing. If Elaine did eventually decide to split with Simon perhaps she might consider moving to Leicester so that they could take a flat together. The nurses' home was a convenient stopgap but you were never really away from the hospital. Although there were no restrictive rules as such, you were not so free an agent as in your own place.

Sister Flint was over her operation and well round from the anaesthetic by the time Nicola took over from Jean the next day.

'Karen's been keeping an eye on her,' drawled Jean, her long limbs propped on the waste-paper basket as she gave her report. 'She's still a bit dopey. And that Mr Armstrong, the new meniscectomy, is asthmatic. Meryl's keeping an eye on him. By the way, did Iris tell you about our idea for the fête?'

'Yes. I hear you've dropped me in it,' said Nicola with a wry grin.

'They demand our bodies as well as our souls!'

'Iris said you suggested it,' accused Nicola.

'I may have done. These bright ideas always rebound, don't they?' Jean sighed with mock resignation and Nicola laughed.

'Go on—go and get your lunch—Legs!' She did a quick tour of the ward to make sure that all was well.

At visiting time Avril Jenkins' mother arrived accompanied by a tall, slim youth. She bustled up to Nicola with an eager smile. 'Nurse, this is Avril's boyfriend, Brian, who was in the accident with her.'

'Hallo, Brian. Glad you're on your feet again,' Nicola beamed.

The lad looked rueful. 'They're hoping I can work some miracle on Avril, but after what I let her in for I wouldn't be surprised if she never wanted to speak to me again.'

'Don't say things like that. I don't suppose she blames you for the accident. Anyway, her leg's going to be OK,' consoled Nicola. 'It just takes a bit of time.'

Seeing Sister Flint's bell lighting up on the nurses' station, she excused herself from the visitors to answer it.

'Hallo, Sister. How are you feeling?'

'So-so, dear. I don't have any water. I'd like a drink.'

'Oh! I expect Millie thought you were still nil-by-mouth. I'll get you some.' Nicola went away and returned with a jug and glass. Putting an arm behind Sister Flint's solid shoulders, she helped her to take a sip. 'I'll do your blood pressure while I'm here,' she said, 'then I'll get Karen to help me sit you up and put on your own nightie.' Fastening the cuff around the sister's muscular forearm, she pumped it up and checked the figures on the sphygmomanometer.

'How is it?' Sister Flint lifted her head to peer at the scale.

'It's fine. Hundred-and-twenty over eighty. We'll give you a nice wash to freshen you up a bit. Be with you in a minute.' Seeking out Karen to help, she came back with a washing trolley and after sponging the sister's face and hands, they removed the theatre gown and replaced it with her own nightdress before remaking the bed.

'I like your plaster bootees,' said Karen brightly as they lifted their patient back against the bed rest and plumped up the pillow under her newly-plastered feet.

Sister Flint studied the workmanship critically. 'Should have thought the plasters would have been higher, but I suppose Tresilian knows what he's doing.'

'You'll get longer ones in ten days' time when we remove your sutures. It's not necessary at this stage because you're not going to be hopping about yet awhile.' Nicola replaced the cradle and they rearranged the covers. 'Is your sister coming to see you?'

'All the way from Edinburgh? Good heavens, no! Hardly a matter of life and death, is it? Nothing to make a fuss about. And I'll be going up there to convalesce.'

'How's the pain?' Nicola enquired.

'I can manage,' returned Sister Flint stoically.

'Well, don't put up with it if it gets too bad. Much better to sleep it off till things settle down.' Making sure that everything was well within her reach, they left her tidying her iron-grey hair.

It was seven o'clock before Mr Tresilian and Alex Baron came up to the ward to see how their operative cases were faring. 'Here comes trouble!' groaned Sophie rolling her brown eyes and she beat a hasty retreat to the sluice room.

Nicola went to greet them. 'Good evening,' she said as they paused outside the side ward.

Tresilian did not deign to reply, but Alex said agreeably, 'Is it convenient to go in?'

'Yes.' She led the way.

Sister Flint lay back against her pillows with eyes closed and lines of pain on her flushed face. She was not asleep and looked up as they entered.

The consultant nodded at her, hands in his

pockets, rocking on the heels of his polished black shoes. 'Behavin' yerself?'

She ignored that remark. 'I hope you've made a good job of this, Hector.'

'Ever known me to mess anything up?' he barked.

'Aye!' she barked back, 'though mebbe not in the field of surgery.'

He frowned under his fierce eyebrows. 'Still the same lovable Hilda. Bet your staff are glad to see the back of you for a while.'

Her flush deepened. 'Still the same hectoring Hector. You always were impossible, even as a student.'

Alex, standing alongside the consultant, hid a grin behind his hand.

Tresilian waved an arm, indicating with an impatient gesture that he wanted to inspect his handiwork.

Nicola turned back the bedclothes over the cradle.

'Splendid job, splendid job,' he boomed. 'How do they feel?'

'How do you think they feel after your butchery?'

He gave a mirthless laugh. 'Ha! You'll soon be terrorising the nurses again.'

'I don't terrorise people. I leave that to you.'

To her dismay Nicola detected a distinct wobble in Sister Flint's chin. Oh no! She couldn't allow ITU's tower of strength to break down in front of them. Quickly replacing the covers she said calmly, 'Perhaps you'll postpone the slanging match till later? Sister's not on top form at the moment.'

There was a stunned silence in the small room as Hector Tresilian's terrier eyes snapped in her direction. Nicola faced his quelling gaze defiantly. She didn't care tuppence for this nasty piece of work.

Tresilian switched his gaze towards Alex. 'Where did you find this one?' he demanded.

'Nurse Pascall, sir? Oh, I picked her up on a train, actually,' said Alex.

The consultant's eyebrows shot up. 'Really! Amazin' what you find on trains.' And he exploded into something resembling a guffaw.

Nicola let them see themselves out of the room. She wasn't going to kowtow to that obnoxious creature. Plumping up Sister Flint's pillows, she said, 'I suppose we must forgive him his rudeness, since he's who he is.'

'His mother should have slapped his bottom years ago,' mumbled the sister. She blew her nose busily. 'I hope that's not true, what he said about me terrorising my staff. One has to see the work's done properly.'

'Well, *his* bedside manner leaves much to be desired, so I shouldn't let it worry you. Now I'm going to insist that you have your pain-killer. You're written up for Omnopon. You know it's a vicious circle, just lying there putting up with things, it only makes matters worse.'

'Thank you, my dear. You're a good girl,' Sister Flint said gratefully.

CHAPTER SIX

MONTFORT Ward seemed to be having more than its fair share of traffic on Friday morning. The mobile X-ray unit trundled in to take fresh pictures of Avril Jenkins' fractured tibia. The path lab ladies were collecting blood samples. On top of a long step-ladder an electrician was replacing a broken bulb. The cleaner was mopping the floor and Millie, the ward-maid, was going round with fresh water jugs. One of the student nurses was off sick and the telephone rang constantly.

In the treatment room Nicola had been supervising Anna in taking out sutures and now they pushed the patient back to bed, bypassing the various obstacles.

'All we need,' said Anna, returning the wheelchair to base, 'is for someone to have a coronary.'

Nicola hastily touched wood. 'Don't tempt providence!'

'It'll either be that or Sister Flint falling out of bed,' cracked the junior.

'She's safe enough at the moment,' Nicola returned. 'Arthur's working on her.'

Arthur, the physiotherapist, was a bluff, grey-haired Yorkshireman with a voice as rich as black treacle and a great way with encouraging patients to use their recalcitrant muscles. Although Sister Flint was confined to bed he was already putting her through isometric exercises to keep her thigh and

110

calf muscles toned up. Nicola had been rather amused to find the austere sister positively coquettish towards him.

Arthur came from Sister Flint's room as Nicola spoke, laughter lines creasing his rugged face.

'Been having fun, Arthur?' she enquired.

'Aye. She's a caution, that one, but I'll lick her into shape before I've finished.'

'I think you could get movement out of an Epstein sculpture, given the time,' observed Nicola with a smile.

Lunches were being cleared away when Alex and Max came to the ward armed with Mr Naylor's X-rays.

'You carry on, don't mind us,' Alex said airily to Nicola, who was making out the pharmacy list. He went to the notes trolley to search out the patient's folder. 'Did you know this girl is a Tresilian-stopper?' he remarked to Max, screening an X-ray plate.

Max stroked his dark beard, studying Mr Naylor's spinal column. 'A *what*?'

'First time I've ever seen our chief at a loss for words. She'd have us believe she's a shrinking violet, but it's not true you know.'

Nicola made a face at his broad back as he carried on talking, pointing out the protruding disc between two of Mr Naylor's vertebrae. 'I've discussed this with Tresilian and we agree a laminectomy is not called for at present. No infection in the spinal fluid and no lesion of the cord. Bed-rest and traction should see him right in about a month.' He turned a wicked glance in Nicola's direction. 'Oh!

You still here? You were so quiet I thought you'd left us.'

There were a great many unmentionables she would have liked to fling at him but it was probably more debunking to say nothing. She carried on with what she was doing.

'I take it you heard what's been decided about Mr Naylor, or are you deaf as well as dumb?'

'Yes, I heard you.' Nicola smiled sweetly at Max before turning a stoney face towards Alex. 'All my faculties are in good working order. You'd like me to see to the traction for you?'

'If you will,' he returned, almost curtly. 'Three kilos on each foot . . . reduced to two kilos at night. We'll go and put him in the picture.'

She stayed to finish her clerking, knowing that she had somehow succeeded in getting under his skin, but it didn't give her a great deal of satisfaction. Her eyes followed the doctors down the ward. They made an odd pair, she thought. Alex dwarfed the lively young Irishman who bounced along beside him as though there were springs to his feet. The registrar's long, muscular legs swung from the hips with a sensual grace. Everything about the man was calculated to inflame the senses, from his gleaming blond head to his purposeful gait. It would do him good to know that here was one person who didn't succumb to his charms.

Keeping an eye on the doctors' movements she waited until they left Mr Naylor and disappeared into Sister Flint's room before dealing with the required traction.

Gathering together weights, pulleys, cords and elastoplast, she called Anna to assist her. With Mr

Naylor already wearing a surgical corset it was a simple matter to fasten the weight-bearing cords to this. 'I expect the doctors explained how it works,' said Nicola. 'Keeping a gentle pull on your spine will, we hope, help the disc to go back into place and the inflammation to subside.'

'Yes. They say it might be a long job, though.' Mr Naylor looked despondent, watching the nurses fixing the pulleys to the foot of the bed over which to pass the cords to hold the weights.

'Better to try this before resorting to surgery,' encouraged Nicola. 'We'll just raise this end of the bed slightly to stop you slipping down. There, is that comfortable?'

'I suppose I'll get used to it.'

'We'll let you off at mealtimes. Remind whoever serves you to disconnect the weights in case they forget.' She thought the patient seemed rather downcast. 'Would you like to see your medical social worker about your finances?'

'Yes, I would really.'

'All right, Mr Naylor, I'll get in touch with her.'

Going back towards the office Nicola saw Mrs Rudkin struggling to open a bottle of cordial with her arthritic hands. She paused to help her and stayed to look out of the open window at the sound of a motor-mower whirring.

'Lovely smell isn't it, new-mown grass?' said Mrs Rudkin sniffing appreciatively. 'Someone's got a shocking cold next door,' she went on with a jerk of her head.

From the adjoining cubicle came the sound of persistent and distressing coughing. Nicola frowned. 'I don't think it's a cold. One of the chaps is asthmatic and the pollen count's high today. Probably your lovely grass getting up his nose.'

She went next door to investigate and found Mr Armstrong leaning on his bed-table, the exhausting coughing and wheezing going on without let-up. She passed him a sputum carton as the coughing culminated in retching. He was too drained to speak. He fell back against his pillows, fighting for breath and looking scared. Nicola felt his pulse, eyeing him with concern. It was rapid and there was an alarming blueness around his mouth and nose.

'All right, love,' she said calmly. 'We'll get you some relief.' Swiftly drawing the curtains around his bed, she pressed his buzzer before pulling out apparatus for the oxygen which was piped to all beds.

Karen arrived in prompt answer to the buzzer. 'Get a Venti-mask,' Nicola said quietly but urgently, 'and then find a doctor. See if Alex Baron is still with Sister Flint,' she suggested when Karen returned post-haste with the mask. She had it in place but it was having little effect on Mr Armstrong's struggle for breath when Alex pushed his way through the curtains.

He made a rapid assessment of the situation and shot a quick glance towards Nicola. 'He'd better have some hydrocortisone IV and 250 mgs of aminophylline, if you'll get that for me.'

Sitting on the side of the bed, he held the facemask for Mr Armstrong. 'Hang on old chap, we'll soon have you feeling more comfortable. Probably a bit of reaction from your op as much as anything.' He carried on talking soothingly while Karen and Nicola hurried to get the equipment and drugs.

Improvement took a little while after the injection and the fixing up of the intravenous drip, but presently Mr Armstrong could breath without the mask and the strain left his face. 'Thank you,' he murmured gratefully.

'Panic over,' Nicola said as she wiped his moist face and rearranged his pillows. She was glad that Alex had been within call. Whatever reservations she might have about him as a man, she could not but admire his skill as a doctor and he had a good way with patients.

The ward was by now full of visitors and Alex said, 'Are you expecting company, Mr Armstrong? They'll be wondering what's going on.'

'Just my wife,' the patient said.

Nicola drew back the curtains. 'Yes, she's waiting outside. I'll send her in.' She went to find the lady. 'He's had a little difficulty breathing, Mrs Armstrong, but he's OK now.'

Going back to the office Nicola was waylaid by a thick-set man in a check shirt, beer-belly protruding over tight navy jeans. 'Where's Mr Naylor, Nurse?' he asked mildly.

She turned to point. 'Third cubicle down,' and she went on to record her notes on Mr Armstrong.

Alex was seated in the office, writing, one muscular thigh crossed over the other in the pose she knew so well, the gold pen flying across the page.

'Excuse me.' He came up behind her as she sat at the desk, leaning over to take a blood test form from the paper rack. His hard cheek brushed the side of her face but there was no apology as she moved slightly to one side. 'I know you'd rather have my room than my company,' he said drily, 'but you called for my assistance so you'll have to put up with me for the time being.'

'I've no views one way or the other,' she said.

'How many fingers have you got crossed?' He moved to look into her face.

'None.'

'In that case we shall have to do something about it. I refuse to be disregarded in this flippant manner.'

'You've no choice, Mr Baron.'

'Mr Baron always has choices—and the name is Alex.'

The eyes that looked into hers were searching and dangerous. She felt her defences slipping away. He had a fatal fascination that made her want his arms to close about her instead of harmlessly supporting his own body by resting either side of her on the desk.

She drew a deep, steadying breath. 'Well then, would you please choose to let me get on with my work?'

He straightened up. 'All right, but I shall return to this discussion at a later date. I'll just check on Mr Armstrong before I go.'

Unwelcome excitement surged through her veins as he disappeared down the ward. What was it about him that turned all her good resolutions topsy-turvy when she knew quite well that it was probably the same with him as with Simon Hill? If you showed no interest then that made you a more desirable property. Maybe if she tried less hard to distance herself from Alex he would lose interest, which would be better for her peace of mind.

Because she was not going to be a notch to anyone's belt. And that was all he probably had in mind.

Tom Woodman's bell rang; also someone else's bell in the same cubicle. There was the sound of shouting. She got up to investigate and saw Karen hurrying down the ward in a state of agitation.

'One of the visitors has gone berserk!' she panted. 'He's tipped a jug of water over Mr Naylor!'

'Oh, my goodness!' exclaimed Nicola.

'Baron said to get the security. He and one of the visitors have got him under control for the moment.'

Nicola hurried back to the office to phone for assistance, before going to see if she could help.

She found two male visitors importantly restraining the man whom Nicola had innocently directed to Mr Naylor's cubicle. Alex mopped at his own bloodied nose while attempting to calm the drenched Mr Naylor, anchored to his bed by traction. His wife stood by, weeping.

'The security men are on their way,' Nicola confirmed.

'What he needs is a ball and chain!' shouted the assailant. 'I'll teach him to steal my wife . . . bloody Casanova!'

'OK, chaps, get him out of here,' urged Alex.

'Righto, Doc,' said one of the visitors, obviously enjoying the scrap. 'Come on, you, on yer bike. Oughter be ashamed of yourself, attacking a poor chap in bed.' They frog-marched him down the ward followed by Alex, by which time the security men had arrived to take charge.

Nicola stayed to pacify the patient. 'Are you all

right, Mr Naylor, apart from being wet? You didn't get hit?'

He shook his head, looking embarrassed. 'Dr Baron got the punch he meant for me. It isn't true, you know. I never touched his wife, honest.'

'Well, that's not any of our business.' She drew the curtains. 'I'll get your bed changed and if you'd like to come with me, Mrs Naylor, we'll find you a cup of tea.'

She escorted the tearful woman to the day room and sent Karen and Anna to change the bed while she made the woman a drink.

'He's our neighbour,' Mrs Naylor gulped. 'He's got this fixation about his wife having affairs while he's away. My husband gives her a lift to the station sometimes, that's all. Oh dear, poor Geoff, he'll be the laughing-stock of the ward, won't he?'

'I don't suppose so,' said Nicola kindly. 'People are much more understanding than you think. It may be possible to transfer him to our other ortho-paedic ward if he feels awkward. Leave it to us. We'll sort something out.' Visiting time had come to an end and people were beginning to drift home-wards. 'You can go in and see your husband again for a while when they've finished making his bed.'

Leaving the woman to get a grip on herself, Nicola returned to her work. Passing the treatment room she saw Alex sitting on a chair pinching the bridge of his nose. She went in to him. 'Can I get you some ice? Let me see the damage.'

He took his hand away and mumbled thickly, 'It's OK . . . I thig it's stobbed now.'

'Gosh! He really has spoiled your beauty.' She

tried to sound solicitous but it was difficult to keep the laughter out of her voice. She ran the cold water tap and wetted a gauze swab, gently wiping the traces of blood from around his nose. 'It's not broken, do you think?' It was no good, she had to giggle.

He scowled at her. 'Maybe I'll get it X-rayed. And it's not funny!'

'It's very serious,' she agreed, and giggled again. 'Shall I kiss it better, or don't you believe in folk medicine either?'

He was still scowling. 'I'll say when I want to be kissed, my girl, and it won't be on my bloody nose, either.'

'Well, if you're sure you don't need a blood transfusion, I'd better go and make out an incident report.' Still fighting against laughter, she left him surveying the damage to his face in the mirror over the sink.

By the time Nicola handed over at four-thirty the commotion had died down and things were back to normal. Later that evening in the Nun's Head the fracas on Montfort Ward was the main talking point.

'No, Alex's nose wasn't broken, just battered,' said Max. 'Can't say I'm sorry I missed the action. If that's what the guy did to superman he'd have flattened me!'

'Glad I wasn't on duty either,' said Meryl with relief. 'Must have been hairy.'

Nicola gave a diffident grin. 'I think the visitors quite enjoyed the sideshow and Alex came off the worst.' She broke into giggles again.

Max looked at her roguishly. 'He told me you

seemed to find it hilarious that he'd been zonked on the hooter.'

'Well, it did kind of spoil his dignity.'

'Y'know, it's a lethal occupation, being a doctor,' put in Joe.

Nicola finished her Coke. 'Oh well, let's hope he doesn't have anything special on this weekend. Like a date with Miss World,' she added mischievously.

'No, his date is with Dora Cromwell,' said Max, 'so he'll be getting plenty of tea and sympathy.'

The subject was dropped in favour of talk about the fête the following weekend. Joe said that Neil would be back and they'd decided on the party at his flat in the evening. Would the girls mind seeing to the snacks? 'Nothing elaborate, you know the sort of thing. I'll give you some cash.'

'OK, I'll rope Iris in,' said Nicola. 'We'll raid Marks.'

Back at the nurses' home she rang Elaine before going to bed. 'How's it going with you and Simon?'

'Blowed if I know,' said her friend morosely. 'We make a date and he fails to turn up. And I'm damn sure his excuses are phoney. Another thing . . . he and Ros are pretty familiar, and I'm going on nights on Monday week which'll take me off the scene.'

Nicola did a quick calculation. 'I think that fits in rather well. You'll have your days off before that. It's going to be a good weekend here. Come down. You can sleep on my floor.'

They agreed that she would meet Elaine at the station the following Friday evening and they parted on a cheerful note. Joe's was the first private party Nicola had been invited to since coming to Priory Cross, but it was not on this little milestone that she dwelt in the moments before she felt asleep. It was of the sun-god with his bloody nose—and his date with Dora Cromwell. Godfather to her daughter he might be, but Nicola felt herself very disapproving of the way he seemed to live in her pocket.

As she went on duty the following day she met Alex leaving the hospital. After his annoyance with her she had expected to receive nothing more than one of his curt nods and was rather surprised when he stopped to talk.

'You shouldn't have any more domestic disturbances,' he said. 'We've transferred Mr Naylor to Jones Ward.'

'Oh, good.' Nicola's gaze took in the bruising spreading across the bridge of his nose, purpling into dark circles beneath his eyes. 'How does it feel?' she asked softly. 'I really am sorry, I shouldn't have laughed.'

'I hope you mean that.' His bland expression belied his severe tone of voice. 'If you do, what do you suggest by way of reparation? Dinner with me tonight?'

'I'm working till nine-thirty.'

'All right, what about tomorrow?'

She hesitated for a moment. Time to put her new theory into practice? Maybe if she stopped being cool to him he would tire of the game. 'Well, I *am* off at four-thirty tomorrow.'

'That will do fine. Do you play tennis?'

'Yes, although I'm not marvellous.'

'You'll do,' he said with a patronising smile. 'My

other guests aren't Wimbledon standard either. I'll pick you up at five.'

He would have sauntered off but she laid a hand on his arm. 'Could you be a bit more explicit? I mean, where are we playing and what do I wear?'

'What do you usually wear? Your birthday suit if you like.'

She tossed her head impatiently, almost losing her cap in the process. 'All right. If you can't be serious I won't come.'

'Oh, yes, you will. This is your penance remember, for mocking the afflicted!'

Putting her headgear to rights, she sighed. 'Is it just tennis things? Do I need a dress for afterwards?'

'You would probably prefer to change for dinner, although it's only at my place. There's a court in my back garden.'

He went on his way leaving her full of curiosity. She was intrigued at the prospect of meeting him socially, wondering who his other guests were, but part of her was scared. Scared because being with him set all her nerves tingling. The set of his shoulders, the way he had of looking at her . . . it confused all her rational reasons for steering clear of anything more than friendship with the opposite sex.

She was right, though. She *had* to be right. Men were deceivers ever, as Shakespeare said. Just because a man had the power to make you remember you were very much a woman didn't mean that you had to lose your head.

Nicola made a firm decision that she was not going to lose hers. Perhaps it would rain, she thought optimistically, and that would wash out his plans.

But the weather held fine. After leaving work on Sunday she quickly showered, put on a brief white tennis skirt and primrose shirt and packed a stripey cotton sun-dress to change into later. It had gone five when she went downstairs with her tennis holdall, wondering if he would be there.

He was. Sitting waiting for her with the sun-roof of his car open, he drummed absently on the steering wheel. His white sports shirt, unbuttoned at the throat, showed the small forest of golden hairs on his chest.

'Hi!' she said, and he turned as she opened the car door and slipped in beside him, dropping her things over onto the back seat.

'Had a good day?' He started up the engine as she settled herself in.

'Fine. All the visitors were on their best behaviour.'

He allowed himself a half-smile. 'So you've got plenty of energy left to run me into the ground, have you?'

'I don't know about that. Hope the others aren't experts. Do I know them, by the way?'

'Yes, one of them. Dora. And the other is Chrissie, her daughter. She's thirteen. You won't mind playing with a schoolgirl, I suppose?'

'Of course not.' Nicola fought back irrational feelings of irritation and resentment. What was he up to? Involving her as some kind of chaperone in his clandestine affairs? 'Where's Mr Cromwell?' she asked abruptly.

'He's away at the moment.'

'Oh!'

'And what did that "oh" imply?'

She watched the passing landscape. 'It didn't imply anything.'

He looked slightly sceptical but did not pursue the subject. 'You'll like Chrissie, she's a nice kid,' he said, 'and you'll be good for Dora too. She's been under the weather lately.'

'I'll do my best to be a ray of sunshine then,' she returned.

'I hope it won't be too much of a strain.' He gave her a sardonic sideways look.

She didn't let it rile her. Why let his sarcasm spoil what might otherwise be an enjoyable game? She'd forget all about personalities and concentrate on putting up a good show.

Nicola had not been back to the locality since the night Simon had driven her out there under a false pretext. Then it had been too dark to see the place properly. Now, as Alex turned the car into his drive, she saw the distinctive gabled residence in all its elegance as it dreamed in the afternoon sunlight. It was indeed much too large for one person, but she could understand how he would hate to leave it.

From the side of the house a slim, long-legged teenager ran round, brown pony-tail caught back with a pink ribbon.

'Hallo!' she said gaily when Nicola got out of the car. 'You're young! He told me you were about a hundred.' She ran up to Alex and aimed a punch at his solar plexus. 'You!'

He doubled up in mock pain and groaned. 'Watch it. I'm injured, don't forget.'

She gave him a look of sheer adoration. 'Pull the other one.'

'This,' he said, putting an arm around Chrissie's shoulders, 'is Nicola. And no, she's not *quite* a hundred.'

Nicola smiled at the youngster. 'He only makes me feel it sometimes.'

'Well, let's go and find your mother, shall we?' said Alex. 'I could do with a long, cool drink.'

'Dora's made some iced lemon.' Chrissie danced ahead round to the back of the house. There were padded garden chairs and a table on the patio and Dora Cromwell appeared from the french windows carrying a tray with a jug and tumblers. She had obviously known who to expect for she expressed no surprise as she greeted her staff nurse.

They sat down to have their drinks. Nicola looked around her at the roses and herbaceous flowers which bordered a sloping lawn, at the bottom of which was a red-surfaced tennis-court. 'What a lovely garden,' she said. 'How do you find the time?'

'I don't do it,' Alex explained. 'I have a man. He was here when my parents were alive. Getting on in years now, I'm sad to say.'

'And his wife's the treasure who keeps the house so beautifully, so Alex is thoroughly spoiled, isn't he?' put in Dora with a fond smile. 'How are you getting on with Sister Flint?' she asked Nicola.

'All plain sailing so far, apart from her verbal clashes with Mr Tresilian, which I gather is standard practice.'

'It's a love-hate relationship,' said Alex with a lazy grin. 'There's a lot of it about.'

'Oh, stop talking about your stuffy old hospital,' said Chrissie. 'I thought we were going to play tennis?'

'So we are, sport.' Alex put down his glass and stripped off his trousers, under which he had a neat pair of brief tennis shorts. 'Come on . . . race you.'

The pair of them ran for the court. Dora and Nicola followed at a slower pace. 'Alex should have children of his own,' Dora said. 'He'd make a lovely father.'

Nicola didn't comment.

They spun racquets for partners and Nicola found herself teamed with the youngster while Dora partnered Alex.

'And don't you give me any soft serves, either!' yelled Chrissie as Alex prepared to serve to her after a knock-up. 'Play properly.'

'Right, young lady. You asked for it.' He unleashed a fierce ball which skimmed the net and went beyond the service line, to her hoots of derision.

After a few preliminary blunders they settled down to an enjoyable and light-hearted game. It resulted in Nicola and Chrissie managing to win the third set. But not, Nicola suspected, without the registrar soft-pedalling. The teenager had been well coached by someone and was a promising young player.

'Are you planning to follow your mother into nursing?' Nicola enquired as she strolled back with Chrissie towards the house.

'Ooh, no! Too much like hard work for me. And look at Alex . . . that bleeper thing of his is always sounding off at the most inconvenient moments. At least when my dad's finished an assignment he's finished.'

'What does your father do?'

'He's in TV. He's away at the moment.'

Back at the house the dining-table was already laid in the large, gracious living-room which looked out over the garden. When they had washed and changed Dora brought in the meal. Cold meats and salad, followed by a raspberry flan and cream. Whether she had prepared it as well Nicola didn't know, but she obviously knew her way around Alex's house.

'I'll make coffee,' said Alex when they had finished eating. He went off towards the kitchen.

Chrissie flopped in an easy chair after turning on the television. Dora gathered up some of the empty dishes and went out after Alex. Nicola decided she ought to do her bit and picked up the remainder of the things to take to the kitchen. She found Alex with his arm around Dora's shoulders and overheard him saying, 'It'll be all right, stop worrying.'

She stood hesitantly in the doorway, feeling like an intruder, wondering if she should discreetly disappear. But they had heard her approach and Alex looked round at her, not the least embarrassed. 'And what are you up to?' he asked.

'I wondered if I could help wash up?'

He took the dishes from her and set them on a working surface. 'Leave it. Chrissie has to get back to school tonight so we'll run this pair home in a minute and then I'll take you back. Go and sit down.'

She did as she was told and made bright conversation with Chrissie. 'Do you live near here?'

'Yes, a couple of streets away. But I'm a weekly boarder at Finchams, worse luck.'

'Where's that?'

'Only about half-an-hour away. I'll be jolly glad when I can leave,' she went on. 'Mummy prefers it like this because her hours aren't regular and Dad's out on location a lot. I'd be perfectly all right at home, you know. Expect they're afraid I'd take boys home or something. But I can't stand boys—I mean, compared with someone like Alex they're the absolute *end*.'

Nicola smiled. 'You prefer them more mature, do you?' Privately she wondered whether having Chrissie out of the way was convenient on other counts, and then despised herself for her uncharitable thoughts. Dora had been quite agreeable to her that afternoon; she had been less twitchy and tense than on the ward. Maybe she had needed the break, and bringing up a spirited daughter like Chrissie without much support from her husband couldn't be all that easy.

The coffee arrived but after sitting down for half a minute, Dora fidgeted. 'Actually we haven't really time to stop for this, Alex. Chrissie will be in hot water if I get her back late.'

'OK.' Alex spread his hands in resignation. 'I'll run you back now. Come on, get your things together,' he hustled the reluctant schoolgirl. 'Stay and have your coffee, Nicola, I shan't be long.'

It was strange, finding herself alone in Alex's house when they had left. She drank her coffee and carried his back to the kitchen. It would need reheating when he returned. Their dishes lay piled by the sink and she thought she might as well at least start the washing up while she waited. She had almost completed the job by the time he returned.

'I told you not to bother with that,' he said, coming up behind her and putting his hands one on each side of her waist.

The action startled her so that she dropped the cup she had been rinsing. Fortunately it bounced.

'Sorry,' she said, stooping to pick it up. 'Hope it's not chipped.'

He took it from her and set it down on the draining board. 'Cups are expendable. Dry your hands and come and tell me the story of your life.' He passed her a towel.

Her whole body was on edge at his nearness. 'There's nothing to tell that would interest you.'

'Let me be the judge of that, Miss Private Person.'

She towelled her hands meticulously, avoiding the blue eyes that watched her, so fascinating in their depth of colour. He was a king-sized specimen of virility. If she stayed there with him for any length of time there was no doubt she would be just as vulnerable to him as were Dora and her young daughter.

'I really think I ought to be going. I'm on an early tomorrow and it's getting late.'

He glanced at his watch and raised an eyebrow. 'Nine-thirty? Late? What you really mean is that you're scared of being here alone with me. Isn't that it?'

'Don't try anything,' she flared, 'or you'll be sorry.'

'Oh yes, I've heard you can take care of yourself.'

'What do you mean?'

'Word gets around,' he said cryptically. He rested his hands, one on either side of her, against the work-surface on which she was leaning, so that she was imprisoned where she stood.

She drew a deep, quivering breath, looking up at his teasing face. She felt the subtle, primitive chemistry flowing between them. The potent power of his body was too close to resist. Her lips parted slightly. He had only to bend his head and her mouth would have yielded to his.

'You're a handful,' he murmured. 'You're enough to make a strong man suicidal.'

That brought her sharply to her senses. He couldn't have said anything more wounding. She was reminded forcibly again of Leo and the feelings of guilt that had compounded her pain, even though she knew she had not been to blame for what happened. She was not going to be swept off her feet a second time.

'I'd like to be getting back, please,' she said with ice in her voice.

He dropped his hands, the teasing mood gone. His own face was as cold as hers. 'OK. Get your things.'

Mustering her dignity, she marched head high into the hall to collect her racquet and bag. Outwardly she was cool, but her heart raced.

They drove in silence back to the hospital.

'Thank you for coming,' he said tersely. 'I hope you enjoyed yourself some of the time.'

'Of course I did. Very much.'

'Liar. One of these days you're going to say that with conviction. Goodnight.'

'Goodnight.' Her face was burning as she opened the car door and waited while he passed her things from the back seat before roaring away. Going to the privacy of her room, she collapsed on the bed, her limbs trembling. Damn the man! He had Dora in his pocket, and probably others. Why then couldn't he leave her alone? So much for her new strategy of making herself available. Never again would she agree to go with him anywhere, for any reason whatsoever . . .

CHAPTER SEVEN

ELAINE's father had been in London on business prior to her weekend with Nicola. He brought her back with him by car and they were able to deliver the remainder of Nicola's belongings to the nurses' home. They all had coffee in her room before he went on to Derbyshire.

'Well, I'll be getting along now,' Mr Garner said. 'Couldn't you pop home before you go back? Your mother's longing for a sight of you. Bring Nicola to lunch on Sunday, eh?'

'OK, Dad,' Elaine kissed him goodbye. 'We'll see if we can fit it in.'

Nicola thought her friend seemed rather moody and after her father left it all came bubbling out of her. 'Simon's leaving the country in a month. He's arranged to do a year's elective in Canada—and he never said a word until now.' She burst into tears, sitting on the end of Nicola's bed. 'H-he says it's pointless me waiting for him b-because he doesn't know where he'll be after that.'

'I'm sorry, Elly.' Nicola put a comforting arm around the girl. 'Perhaps it's better this way though. Simon's a bit of a rolling stone, isn't he?'

'Oh, I know you never saw eye to eye with him,' said Elaine, between sniffs. 'I don't know what went on between you that weekend he was up here, but your name was mud.'

'Well, you know me. I never have liked the way

132

he messed you around. Expect he felt my anti-
pathy. I know you must feel pretty sick at the
moment, but maybe it's time you moved on too.
You wouldn't have much difficulty finding a new
job . . . theatre nurses aren't two-a-penny.'

Elaine blew her nose. 'I'll think about it.'

'About tomorrow,' Nicola went on, ''fraid I've
only got a half-day, but I'm off on Sunday so we
could go to see your folks if you'd like. C'mon,
cheer up! We'll go over to our local now and I'll
introduce you to some of the crowd. There's a party
on tomorrow night, after the fête, so you'll meet
some of them again then.'

She and Iris had shopped that afternoon and
bought French bread and various cheeses, pâté and
biscuits, crisps and nuts, leaving the drinks to Joe
and his friends.

Over at the Nun's Head they found Neil,
amongst others. He had just completed the first
week of his new appointment. Nicola made the
introductions. 'How's it going, Neil?' she asked.

'I'm feeling my way,' he said with a cautious
smile. 'How's that young lass on your ward? Is she
speaking yet?'

'Avril? No improvement so far.'

'Ah well, something will spark off recovery in
time. Forgive us talking shop,' he said, turning with
a friendly grin to Elaine.

'Oh, that's all right. I'm used to it. Occupational
hazard in this game, isn't it?'

'In the business are you?'

'Yes, I'm at the Heathside.'

'That's where Nicky and I met, but I don't
remember seeing you there?'

'Well, you wouldn't. I'm in theatre, but not the ENT block.'

Conversation veered to talk of the forthcoming fête. Others joined them and after a convivial evening the girls went back to Nicola's room and bed.

'You can crawl in with me if you like,' Nicola offered.

'No, I've got my sleeping-bag. I'll be all right on the floor.'

'OK, I'll be away before you wake up I expect. Be back at one, though.'

The following morning she dressed as quietly as possible so as not to disturb her sleeping friend, then skipped over to the hospital to join the freshly starched dawn patrol and her own batch of life's casualties. Her first job after the essential chores were out of the way was to remove Sister Flint's stitches.

The sister had been seen by Tresilian on his round late the previous afternoon.

'Right, you can get those plasters removed and the sutures out tomorrow,' he had growled. 'Then let's see how you get on with crutches. Expect you'll fall flat on your face.'

By this time Hilda was equal to anything the irascible consultant could throw at her. 'Fortunately I've got complete faith in my physiotherapist,' she countered. 'I don't anticipate any problems.'

'Huh! I don't envy him. But if he can get you on your feet maybe he can get you walking to church by the time we both retire.'

She looked at him, her darting grey eyes equivocal. 'A backhanded proposal? In front of witnesses too!'

Alex raised an eyebrow in Nicola's direction. She curbed a smile.

Tresilian was looking enormously pleased with himself. 'Don't count your chickens.' He swept on to see the rest of his patients.'

'So the old devil's got round to it at last,' said Alex dryly as he later wrote up the latest developments on case notes.

'She'll need her brains tested if she takes him on,' retorted Nicola.

'Don't you believe in marriage?'

'I didn't say that. It's all right for some people.'

'But you've never got to the point of wanting to?'

'I didn't say that either. What about you? I suppose you prefer other men's wives.'

His eyes had glinted dangerously. 'They certainly don't have such vivid imaginations as one girl I could mention.' He had walked out on her then, leaving her knowing she had handled it badly. Why did she always let him goad her into attack?

This morning, having sent for the plaster technician to remove the old plasters, she wheeled Sister Flint through to the treatment room. The casts were sawn through and lifted off. The skin underneath was scaly and flaked with dried blood over the big toe joints, but the wounds were clean and well knitted and without any inflammation.

'He's made a good job of them,' admitted the sister, casting a critical eye over her feet.

'Yes, he knows his job, even if tact is not his strong point.'

Sister Flint said nothing, watching eagle-eyed as Nicola carefully snipped and extracted the sutures.

'Well done,' she said when it was over. 'You've been well trained, my dear.'

'We'd better let Alex see them before you have your new plasters on. I think he's on Jones at the moment.' Nicola went to phone and when she returned she found Arthur sitting on a stool talking to Hilda.

'Look fine, don't they?' said Arthur. 'You've got good healing flesh for a woman of your years.'

'I'm not that ancient, I'll have you know!'

'Now, now!' the physiotherapist chided. 'This is Arthur you're speaking to. The chap who's going to teach you to walk again, remember?'

'And how long's that going to take?'

'Soon as your new plasters are dry we'll have you in the perpendicular. On the crutches for about six weeks . . . after that it's up to you. Be three months before you're back in harness though.' He patted her hand in a fatherly fashion. 'Never mind, my lovely, I won't desert you.' Her tight mouth relaxed into a smile. '*That's* the ticket,' said Arthur. 'You look no more than twenty-one when you're cheerful.'

'Away with you,' she said, but she smiled again.

Alex arrived and pronounced himself satisfied with the feet. The plaster technician went ahead to apply knee-length plasters.

'They'll take a good couple of days to dry before you can put any weight on them,' warned Nicola. 'Then as soon as you're confident on the crutches, you'll be away. Will you be staying in your room?'

'No, I'll be going to my sister's.'

'Oh, great. It would be a bit dull for you in the nurses' home, although you'd have plenty of visitors I expect.' Nicola wheeled the sister back to her room. 'Not long now and you'll be mobile.'

After tidying up the treatment room she returned to the office. Alex had been checking on his other cases and looked in to write an X-ray form for a Pott's fracture.

'Don't look so worried, it may never happen,' he said as, frowning, she reached for a dictionary.

'I'm not worried. I can't think how to spell metatarso-phalangeal—spelling not being my strong point.'

He obligingly spelt it out for her. 'You'll be shot of the dear lady soon.'

'She hasn't been much trouble. In fact I feel rather sorry for her in a way.'

'Be warned then, if you don't want to end your days similarly.'

'My feet are in perfect condition, thank you.'

'It wasn't your feet I was thinking of.'

She gave him a cold glance although his probing gaze caused a flutter in her throat. 'You're very keen on giving advice,' she said, resuming her writing. 'I'm quite capable of running my own life without advice from you or anyone.'

'And you're quite capable of making a hash of it. The moment a guy gets within spitting distance of you, down come the shutters quick enough to gut his gonads.'

The analogy tickled her sense of the ridiculous. She stifled the giggle that threatened to break surface.

'You,' she said, 'are the most obnoxious, self-opinionated man I have ever met.'

He laughed. 'At least it got me a reaction.'

Balling a piece of paper, she shot it after his departing back.

Elaine had got herself up and tidied the room by the time Nicola returned at one o'clock. She found her being entertained by Iris, whom she had met the previous evening.

'I'm beginning to get cold feet about this kissing booth business,' Iris said with an agonised expression. 'Wonder what our customers will be like . . . or even if we'll get any? We'll probably end up with stinking colds or foot-and-mouth or something.'

'It's only for an hour,' Nicola told Elaine. 'You'll be able to amuse yourself till then, won't you? And afterwards we'll be getting ready for the party.' She stripped off her soiled uniform, dumped it in the linen basket and put on her dressing-gown while they ate a light lunch together in Iris's room.

'Fancy having to get back into uniform on your afternoon off!' Iris groaned.

Shortly before three they wandered over to the field behind the tennis-courts. A carnival atmosphere prevailed. Bunting fluttered in the breeze. Stirring music came from the central arena where a military band was about to finish its performance. Side stalls were doing a brisk trade in coconut shies, roll-a-coin, treasure hunts, pot-plants and the like. Children bounced up and down on an inflated Disney-like castle, while across the tannoy a compère announced that there would shortly be a demonstration of police dogs at work. Gas-filled balloons sailed off into the blue and ice-creams melted in the sun.

Elaine went to browse over a book stall while Nicola and Iris met up with Jean and took over their positions on the kissing booth. On a small platform surrounded with bunting there were three dressings trolleys, each with a collecting box. A white-coated houseman with a stethoscope round his neck urged passers-by to try the restorative qualities of a little affection. 'Roll up! Roll up!' he shouted. 'Kissing is good medicine. And here we have three of the best exponents in the business.'

There were no lack of takers as people drifted away from the military band area. Several ex-patients were amongst Nicola's customers, one being Gil Stevens, walking moderately well.

'First time I've had to pay for the privilege,' he said, putting his coins in the box before giving her a rather shy peck on the cheek.

Nicola smiled to herself. He was not the great ladies' man he would have everyone believe. 'How's the knee?' she said.

'Not so dusty.' He grew a little bolder. 'Can I have another go?'

'Cost you another twenty pence.'

He fished in his pocket, made with the money, and this time gave her a boyish kiss on the lips.

'Move along there,' said her next customer, a sophisticated sixth former who proved to be much more expert.

All in all it was an amusing experience, despite the occasional lecher and the second-hand flavours of beer, garlic and tobacco, but the girls were not sorry when the end of their stint drew near.

Their time was almost up when Alex Baron sauntered by. 'Come on, sir,' urged the houseman, 'we're just about to shut up shop, but we'll make an exception in your case.'

With a one-sided grin, he stepped up onto the platform. Nicola's knees threatened to buckle. She leaned against her trolley, assuming indifference, but colour flooded her cheeks and the butterflies in her stomach wore football boots.

He started with Jean, slipping a pound note into her tin and giving her a brief but firm salute on the lips. He treated Iris in the same way, whispering something which caused her to giggle. Nicola geared herself for a dose of the same as he moved towards her. Diving into his pocket, he found another note, folded it very deliberately and slipped it into her tin. He stood and looked at her for a second, his eyes appraising as she waited with increasing tension. Then he cupped her chin in his hands, held his chiselled mouth half an inch from hers and murmured, 'I'm not buying kisses from *you*. I'm prepared to wait until they're freely given.'

Half-angered, half-relieved, she gritted her teeth when he released her. 'Then you'll have a long wait,' she said in a low voice.

'We'll see.' With an infuriating smirk, he stepped down and went on his way.

That their lips had not met, the other girls seemed not to have noticed.

'Wow!' said Iris, dreamy-eyed, 'Good job they weren't all like him. I should become a confirmed nymphomaniac.'

'Mm! Me too!' agreed Jean.

'Thanks, girls, you've done all right,' their watch-dog remarked, feeling the weight of the collection boxes. 'Do I get kisses for free?'

Parting on a laugh, Iris and Nicola drifted off to find Elaine. They found her at a refreshment table, sitting with Neil, both chatting away like old friends. Nicola had not seen her looking so relaxed and happy for months. But then Neil had that effect on people; he was your genuine twenty-two carat type.

'Hallo, girls, I passed your stand.' He rose and pulled forward chairs for them. 'You seemed to be doing a roaring trade so I decided you could do without my support. Would you like a cuppa? I'll get them.'

Elaine watched with a smile on her face as his long legs loped towards the lady with the tea urn. 'He's nice. He's offered to pick us up for the party tonight, but I didn't know what arrangements you'd made.'

'Well, I have got my own car,' Iris said, 'but if he wants to be chauffeur, why not?' And so it was agreed that Neil would pick them up at eight, since they had the food to take over.

The house which Joe occupied with three other medics was similar in size to that owned by Alex. Each had their own bed-sit upstairs but they shared the large, communal living area on the ground floor. Furniture had been placed against the walls and carpets rolled back. The girls arranged their goodies on the table which had been pushed into one corner. The fellows sorted bottles and cans and glasses and looked out tapes for the music.

Other guests began to drift in and soon the walls

were reverberating to the swell of pop music and the interchange of carefree small talk. Nicola was glad to see Elaine continuing in the same cheerful mood that had started at the fête. She evidently found much in common with Neil. Iris was continuing her pursuit of Joe, who didn't even realise he was being pursued. Not that Iris was seriously enamoured. She had too many personal ambitions to want more than a passing diversion.

For Nicola there seemed to be something lacking in the evening. She found herself wondering whether Alex would put in an appearance, torturing herself as to how to treat him if he did. Time wore on and there was no sign of him. Dancing with Joe, she said fairly casually, 'I'm surprised not to see Alex, since he lives so near.'

'Oh, he was invited, but he had another date.'

Joe's explanation left her feeling as flat as yesterday's lager. For the rest of the evening thoughts of the provoking registrar continued to haunt her. She speculated as to who his date might be. He had been at Priory Cross for some time; his life pattern was established long before she had arrived on the scene. Despite his jibes her existence could have made little difference to him. As if it were of any importance to her anyway. Nevertheless, she felt strangely bereft, as though an important part of her were missing.

It was almost three before the party began to break up. Neil ran the girls back to the nurses' home. 'I'll be in touch, Elaine,' he said in parting.

'What's he going to be in touch about?' Iris wanted to know.

'Oh, just some information he promised to get me,' returned Elaine evasively. 'We'll have to catch a train about eleven tomorrow if we're to get to my place for lunch, Nicky.'

'Well, that gives us a bit of a lie-in.'

Iris yawned. 'You should be so lucky. I'm on an early tomorrow.'

They retired to their rooms. Nicola set her alarm and the girls slept soundly until it woke them. A phone call to Elaine's home assured them of being met at the other end of the line, where her family made Nicola welcome. It made her realise how much she had been missing a taste of home life and she longed for the time when her own parents would be back in England. At present she felt as though she had no real roots anywhere.

After a traditional Sunday roast lunch they drove to a local beauty spot and went for a leisurely ramble in the lovely Derbyshire Dales.

'We were in the grip of winter when I was last home. I'd forgotten how good it can be here,' Elaine said.

'Can't you persuade her to leave London, Nicky?' prompted Mrs Garner. 'Plenty of good hospitals up here she could go to.'

'I do my best,' said Nicola, 'but she takes no notice of me.'

Elaine had brought her overnight bag with her since she was to go straight back to London. After a late tea they reluctantly caught the local train back to Leicester where Elaine changed for the main line service and Nicola made her own way back to the nurses' home.

On Monday Sister Cromwell was back in harness, although not looking a great deal better for her break.

'How's your daughter?' Nicola asked brightly.

'Fine. She wasn't home this weekend. There were a lot of things on at the school. A sports day on Saturday and a confirmation service on Sunday with a strawberry tea afterwards. I've been feeling queasy ever since.' She rubbed a hand over her stomach. 'Alex got us both second helpings. That's what comes of being a piggy.'

Alex, Alex, Alex! Nicola could have screamed. It was almost as though Dora deliberately quoted his name to assert her right to him.

She raised a smile. 'Lovely day though, wasn't it? I went home with a friend of mine to Derbyshire. It was great there.'

They talked of ward matters. 'Sister Flint seems to be on the home stretch, I'm glad to say.' Dora gave a tight smile. 'Arthur's going to get her on her crutches tomorrow. He seems to handle her well.'

'Yes, I've noticed they hit it off. Which is more than you can say for Tresilian.'

'*That* man!' Dora snorted. 'The sooner he retires the better. She's on a bedpan at the moment. Make sure she's not forgotten. By the way, I thought stocks were a bit low when I got back this morning.'

Nicola looked surprised. 'There was sufficient when I went off on Saturday.'

'Oh well, it's better to have too much than not enough. You never know when there's going to be a run on things. I'll order up when I get back from lunch. Two admissions this afternoon. Mr Moore, total hip replacement, and Bridget King, eleven years, another hallux valgus. Case histories on the desk. Give the patients' post out, will you? I simply haven't had the time.'

Nicola distributed the letters before starting work. There were two more get-well cards to add to Avril's vast collection plastered to the wall behind her bed. 'Here you are, love. Someone asked after you the other day. Remember Dr Chadwick who came to examine your throat? He was quite disappointed when I told him you hadn't sworn at us yet.'

Avril smiled, shook her head and sighed.

'Don't worry about it, kid. He says it'll happen spontaneously one day.' Nicola went on to see to Sister Flint. She peeped through the curtains which were drawn around the bed. 'Hallo there, are you ready yet?'

'Yes, my dear, and I'll be verra glad to see the back of these things,' the sister added as Nicola removed the offending object.

'Not long now and you'll be walking to the bathroom. I'll be back with a washing bowl. Pressure areas OK?'

'Oh yes, I've got plenty of padding. Too much, Arthur says, the impudent rascal.' She smiled wryly at some private thought.

Visitors were arriving and with them came the first of the new patients, the little girl to have her bunions fixed. She was small for her age and looked extremely apprehensive, her eyes round and anxious behind her straight fringe.

'Hallo, Bridget,' Nicola greeted her warmly. 'You come with me and your mum can help you undress, but you don't have to get into bed yet if you don't want to.' She led mother and daughter to the bay where Avril was. 'This is Avril. She won't be able to talk to you because she's got a bad throat as well as a broken leg. But she's good at writing things down, and you can talk to her, can't you?' She left the newcomers admiring Avril's many greetings cards.

'You can go and take some notes on Bridget while her mother's here,' Nicola said to Anna. 'She'll be a good subject for your patient assess- ment.'

'Bunions at her age?' Anna frowned. 'Is it bad shoes?'

'Oh no, not always. It can be a hereditary con- dition. Make out her charts and don't forget the identity band on her wrist.'

Sister Cromwell had returned from lunch but had taken herself off somewhere, leaving the rest of the staff to cope with the ward and visitors' enquiries.

Bridget's mother approached Nicola before leaving. 'How long do you think she'll be in, Nurse?'

'Is there anyone at home all day?'

'Yes, I don't go out to work.'

'Probably about a week then, just until the pain's under control. But she won't be able to put her feet to the ground and she'll have to be in a wheelchair until her first change of plasters.'

'I see. When's she being done?'

Nicola ran her finger down the operating list. 'In the morning. If you ring up after twelve we'll be able to tell you how she is.'

The mother smiled stoically. 'OK. She's a good little girl, she shouldn't be any trouble.'

'We'll look after her, Mrs King. It makes a

change to have a nice young face in the ward. You have signed the consent form, I suppose?'

'Yes, we did that when we saw the doctor.'

'Right, that's fine.'

Dora Cromwell reappeared as the last of the visitors left and patients were having their afternoon tea. She looked a little pale as she seated herself at the desk and prepared to do some clerking. 'You and the rest of the second shift had better take your break, Nicola.'

'Fine.' Nicola paused before leaving. 'Are you feeling all right, Dora? You look a bit washed-out.'

'Oh, I've got gut-rot. I've had a couple of codeine. Expect I shall last out until you get back.'

Leaving Sophie, two students and an auxiliary to start pressure care and washings, Nicola went to tea with Anna and Karen. Alex's upright figure was disappearing into Jones Ward as they passed. She had not seen him since he'd declined to kiss her at the fête. Remembering that humiliation, she hoped he would have visited Montfort and gone again by the time she returned. And yet she could not deny that he held a certain attraction for her. There was something about him she found hard to resist.

Karen snapped her fingers. 'Wake up at the back there!'

Nicola laughed. 'What did you say? I was miles away.'

'Two of Hilda's staff nurses popped in to see her. They wanted to know what we'd done to tame the old girl.' She assumed a foreign accent. 'We have ways of making zem behave, I told them.'

'More likely to have been Arthur's attentions.

She'll probably be the same old Hilda once she gets back on ITU.'

They returned to the ward twenty minutes later and set about the evening routine. Gathering up some flowers to be put in water, Nicola searched for a vase in the kitchen. On the way back with them she caught sight of Dora in the stock room. She was leaning against a low cupboard, one hand on her stomach, her face contorted with pain.

Hastily Nicola set down the vase and went to her assistance. 'Sister! What's wrong?' The woman was colourless, her upper lip beaded with perspiration.

'Come on, get your head down!' Nicola grabbed her arm to help her towards a chair, but Dora didn't make it. Her legs buckled and she slithered to a heap on the floor.

'Oh God! I . . . feel awful . . .' she moaned, beginning to shiver.

'Can you get to the chair?' Nicola had her hand on the sister's pulse. It was rapid and thready. 'No, better stay where you are.' She called to Sophie who was passing. 'Bring a pillow and a blanket, Sister's not well.'

Sophie hurried to help and they tucked the pillow behind her head and covered her with the blanket. Dora was taking deep, sighing breaths. Even her hands were the colour of parchment. The nurses looked at each other, alarmed. This was more than an upset tummy—it seemed more like an internal haemorrhage.

Dora confirmed their thoughts. 'Perhaps I'm going to abort. Missed my second period.' She was showing signs of air-hunger and was obviously in acute pain.

'Get some help, Soph,' urged Nicola.

'Find Alex,' sighed Dora weakly.

'Find anybody!' Kneeling by her side, Nicola held her hand. 'All right, Dora. You're in the right place for treatment anyway.' She noticed the colourless nails. 'Are you losing down below?'

'A bit, not much.' It seemed an effort to speak.

Sophie had found Alex coming from Jones Ward.

'She thinks she may have been pregnant,' murmured Nicola looking up at him when he strode into the stockroom.

He took one glance at Dora's chalk-white face. 'Get some transport in here. She'd better go to Casualty. Have you there in a jiffy, Dora,' he said gently, scooping her up in his arms.

Nicola ran for the trolley in the corridor. Wasting no time they rushed the sick woman through passages to the Accident and Emergency department. Meanwhile Sophie phoned through to tell them what to expect.

Leaving Dora with the sister in charge and Alex having a word with the casualty officer, Nicola went back to her ward. The news had quickly swept through the staff.

'*Is* it a miscarriage?' asked Karen.

'She wouldn't be *that* colour,' said Sophie. 'More like an ectopic or a perforated ulcer perhaps—she's always uptight.'

'What's an ectopic?' Anna asked.

'The foetus develops in the Fallopian tube instead of the uterus,' said Nicola. 'It always happens early on in pregnancy. It eventually ruptures the tube and you get an internal haemorrhage.'

But the question that buzzed around her brain was why Sister Cromwell had asked for Alex in particular? If she *was* pregnant—who had been responsible? Alex?

CHAPTER EIGHT

IT WAS not until after eight that Alex paid a return visit to Montfort Ward, primarily to see the new patients for tomorrow's list.

'How is Dora?' Nicola enquired. 'We heard she'd been taken to theatre for investigation.'

'Oh, it was an ectopic,' he said. 'They did a surgical repair and got some blood into her.'

'We thought it might be. She's all right, is she?'

He nodded, concentrating on Mr Moore's case notes. 'She went to Stopes. Expect she'd welcome a visit in a day or two.'

'Did they send for her husband?'

'No, contacted her parents. Dora didn't want him troubled.'

'Oh? That's odd. How long's he been away?' asked Nicola casually.

He closed the folder and leaned back in his chair, fixing her with a long, discerning stare before answering. Her cheeks flushed as she became aware that he had read her thoughts. 'He's been away a month,' Alex said with slow deliberation. 'Dora was eight weeks pregnant. Does that satisfy you?'

She busied herself trying to add up a fluid chart and failed. 'I should have thought he'd want to know, that's all.'

His mouth worked to restrain a smile. 'Well, well! Aren't you ashamed of yourself?'

151

'Why should I be?' she returned, forcing herself to meet his eyes. 'Are you?'

He chose not to answer that. 'I'll be magnanimous and forgive your uncharitable thoughts. You probably felt threatened.'

'What do you mean? Why should I feel threatened?'

'Good question,' he said with infuriating composure. 'Why don't you ask yourself? You might get a revealing answer.'

'Oh, very funny.' She stalked away from him. Conceited ass! As if it mattered to her how he conducted his life.

All the same, although she was furious, his comments hung like a question mark in the air. Had she misjudged him? She'd be glad if she had, because in spite of everything, it was reassuring to find that the sun god did not have feet of clay. But as to feeling threatened . . . if he thought her suspicions had been prompted by jealousy, he was wrong. He was a virile and fascinating man, and his attentions to Dora might lead anyone to a wrong conclusion. He had probably only said what he did to annoy her, she decided. Best to ignore it and have as little to do with him as possible.

But that was easier said than done when work dictated otherwise. He sought her out again before leaving. 'Young Bridget seems a bit tearful. I've done my best. You might try getting your busy brain to work in that direction.'

She gave him a frosty glance. 'No need for sarcasm. We'll do our best to put her at ease.'

'Fine. She's first down, so she won't have long to dwell on it in the morning. I'll write her up for some night sedation. Don't want her to lie there worrying. Now Mr Moore, we'll have to put off his op for a day or two. He seems to have a urinary infection. I've put him on a broad spectrum antibiotic and we'll see how he goes.'

'Are we to keep him in?'

'Oh yes. It won't do him any harm to rest the leg.'

'OK. Anything else?' She wished he would go. Standing there, with his lustrous fair hair framing his strong features, his deep voice stirring complicated emotions within her, it was altogether too much for her to cope with. Too unsettling.

'Plenty, but nothing that we can sort out here and now.' With that enigmatic statement he left her.

Karen came to ask for help with changing Avril's bottom sheet and ward matters asserted their priority. As they finished, Bridget returned from the bathroom. Her eyelids were pink and her bottom lip tremulous.

'Going to get into bed now, love?' Karen said cheerfully. 'Drinks'll be coming round in a minute.'

The child certainly looked woebegone. Nicola had a sudden inspiration. 'Oh, just a minute before you get out of your dressing-gown, Bridget. Come with me, there's someone I'd like you to meet.'

Holding her by the hand she took her along to the side ward and knocked before entering. Sister Flint was laying on top of her bed reading, her new plasters almost dry at last. She looked up as they entered. 'Hallo, who've we got here?'

'This is Bridget, Sister,' Nicola said, flashing eye signals. 'She's having her bunions done tomorrow. I thought she'd like to see how well you've got on. Don't mind, do you?'

'Not at all.' The paragon of ITU put out a hand and patted the chair beside her bed. 'Come and sit down, dear. Here, have one of my jellies.' She waved Nicola away. 'You go and get on with your work. We'll have a little chat.'

It had been a spur-of-the-moment hunch, but Sister Flint had been so agreeable of late it was unbelievable. She'd had vast experience in dealing with scared people in her time and she was probably flattered that she had been asked to help. Nicola smiled and left them to it.

Some moments later Bridget came back looking happier. 'She let me sign my name on her plasters, and she's going to sign her name on mine. There's a man called Arthur who's going to show her how to manage the crutches tomorrow. She says she wishes she'd had hers done a long time ago.'

'I bet she does,' returned Nicola, 'but when she was a little girl doctors weren't so clever as they are today. You're lucky.'

'Will you be here tomorrow, when it's time?'

'Yes, Bridget. And either Karen or I will stay with you until you're fast asleep. Next thing you know you'll be back here in the ward and it'll all be over. Now, you go and clean your teeth and then pop into bed.'

From then on there was too much to do to dwell on personal matters but going back to her room at nine-thirty, thoughts of Alex returned to bedevil her. The more Nicola dwelt on it the more she realised that she could have been wrong about him and Dora. After all, no one else had commented and hospital staff were not slow to spot any goings-on. Perhaps it had all been in her own mind. It made her feel wretched. Tomorrow she would go and see Dora by way of making amends.

After her duty the following day Nicola bought some roses in the florist shop in the entrance hall and took them along to Stopes Ward. Sister Cromwell was propped in a semi-upright position, a blood transfusion taped to her left arm. She had some colour in her cheeks now but still looked wan after her traumatic experience.

'Thank you all for looking after me,' Dora said listlessly as Nicola put the flowers on the bed and sat down beside her. 'Gosh! I have never felt so ghastly in all my life. I really thought I was going to die.'

'You had us worried for a while. I'm awfully sorry about you losing the baby. Were you very disappointed?'

'We-ell, actually, no,' Dora gave a fleeting smile, 'although I wouldn't have chosen it to happen this way. My husband didn't know I was pregnant . . . he wouldn't have wanted another child, anyway.' She paused and gave a heartfelt sigh.

'Have they told Chrissie where you are?'

'Alex phoned the Head, but I said not to alarm her since they're in the middle of exams. She'll have to stay at school again this weekend. Alex said he might try to take her out on Sunday. He's been a tower of strength.'

Dora was silent for a moment. 'You don't know, I suppose, about my problem?'

'What problem?' Nicola asked.

'My husband's an alcoholic.'

'Oh! No, I didn't know.'

The sister bit her lips. 'I like to keep it quiet

because of Chrissie. She thinks he's away working
at the moment, but he's not. He's in a clinic being
dried out. I don't know how I'd have coped without
Alex.'

No wonder Dora lived on her nerves! No wonder
she was fond of Alex—he was probably the one
person she could turn to. Those little touches
of affection she had misinterpreted had been
prompted by sympathy . . . Nicola saw it all
now. Alex was right. She should be ashamed of
herself for thinking otherwise.

'I'm sorry. It must be very difficult for you. Look,
if there's anything ever I can do . . .'

'Oh, we get by,' said Dora with resignation.
'Keep it under your hat, won't you? I wouldn't like
everyone to know, but I felt you'd understand.' She
began to talk of ward matters. 'Don't know how
long I shall be off. Have they sent you any extra
help?'

'They've promised us an Agency nurse.'

'That's all right then, I don't have to worry about
getting back.'

'No, you get properly fit first. I'll be in to see you
again sometime.'

Outside Dora's room Nicola collided with Alex,
about to go in. 'Hallo!' His blue eyes were scathing.
'What's this, an act of contrition?'

She felt rather small but it was more than she
could do to admit it. 'You seem to know all the
answers so think what you like.' On her dignity, she
pushed past him, ruffled but rebellious where he
was concerned.

For Dora she felt tremendous sympathy. You
never knew the pressures which made people act

the way they did. She had guessed there was some kind of problem, only she had jumped to the wrong conclusion. The trouble was, Alex knew that she had. Damn him and his mind-reading act! Life at Priory Cross would be fine and uncomplicated if it weren't for him. Well, she was due for night duty the following week. With a bit of luck their paths might not cross for a while.

It was Thursday before she saw him again. He came to the ward with Max and Hector Tresilian to check up on their post-operative cases. Jean Arden trailed after them with the notes trolley. Nicola herself had wheeled young Bridget to the bathroom and now, as they returned and she was lifted onto her bed, Bridget looked alarmed at the doctors' approach.

'It's all right,' murmured Nicola, 'they're probably coming to tell you when you can go home.' She stayed with the child as the team paused at the foot of the bed.

Tresilian took a brief glance at the temperature chart. 'Everything all right here? Pain under control?' he growled.

'No complaints, have you, Bridget?' Alex gave the youngster a broad wink and she smiled back shyly.

'Anyone at home to look after you?' barked the consultant, not unkindly.

'Yes, my mum.'

He looked at her over the rim of his spectacles. 'You mustn't walk on those feet, you know. You'll have to use a wheelchair until we see you again in ten days' time.'

She swallowed and nodded dumbly.

'Right. She can go. Make an outpatient appointment for her.' Tresilian swept on to the next bay.

'There, what did I tell you?' Nicola lowered her voice. He's not so bad, is he? Only sounds a bit grumpy.'

'I like Dr Baron best. Can I go today?' Bridget asked excitedly.

'Probably. We'll have to ring your mummy and see when it's convenient.'

'I'm beating Sister Flint, aren't I? She hasn't got a mum to look after her, but Arthur's going to drive her to Scotland to see her sister when she's good on her crutches. She likes Arthur, doesn't she?'

Nicola grinned. 'It would seem so,' she agreed.

She was in Sister Flint's room straightening her bed when the consultant and his team made that their last port of call.

'I see you're managing all right on those things,' Tresilian said brusquely, watching as the sister balanced while putting something away in her locker before giving him her full attention.

'There's not much stumps me,' she said.

'And what do you propose to do with yourself if I give you your marching orders?'

'Friend of mine is going to look after me.'

'Huh! I wish her joy,' Tresilian grunted.

'*He* seems to think it'll be a privilege.'

The consultant was at a loss for words, but only momentarily. 'He must be a saint then. See you in my clinic in six weeks.'

Sister Flint chuckled as he left. 'That foxed him,' she said.

Nicola laughed. 'Bridget told me you were being escorted up north. When are you going?'

'End of the week. Yes, it's very kind of Arthur. He's got some holiday—going to stay with relatives in Edinburgh. Says he'll be glad of the company.' Her plump face coloured a little. 'You've all been verra good to me, but I shan't be sorry to leave.'

When Nicola went back to the main ward Tresilian and Max had gone but Alex still lingered in the office, where he was screening Avril's latest X-ray. 'I think our Hilda surprised the boss,' he said with a brief glance in her direction.

'Thought he was the only pebble on the beach, did he?' returned Nicola in a mild tone. 'He'll have to watch it. Arthur and Sister Flint have built up quite a rapport.' She watched him as he studied another X-ray, thoughtfully scratching the side of his cheek.

Feeling her eyes upon him, he turned with a look of enquiry. 'Something on your mind?'

'Oh, no. Well, that is, Dora said you might be taking Chrissie out on Sunday.'

His eyebrows lifted fractionally. 'Yes, I thought I might, since her father's still away and the grandparents have to go back. Why?'

'Well, um, I'm free on Sunday. Would it help if I came along?'

The mesmeric blue eyes bored into hers. 'If you'd like to come, we'd be glad to have you. What brought about this change of heart?'

She didn't know quite why she offered, unless it was because he still kept Dora's secret and didn't attempt to explain his motives. 'I like the kid,' she said, 'and I'm going onto nights on Monday so I might not be around to help for a while.'

'Sunday it is then. We'll pick you up—say two-thirty?'

Nicola left the ward that night feeling glad to have made a kind of truce with him.

The telephone in the corridor rang as she and Iris were having coffee together. Iris bounced up. 'I'll go, Joe said he might ring.' She came back a few seconds later looking disappointed. 'Your friend Elaine. *She* sounds full of beans, anyway.'

Elaine certainly was. 'Got an interview at Neil's hospital next week, Nick.'

'You have? How did that come about?'

'He promised he'd put in a word for me, but I didn't know whether he meant it, or that it would be so soon. Great, isn't it?'

'Great,' agreed Nicola. 'I was hoping we might get to share a flat again sometime, but you couldn't commute from there.'

'Well, at least we'd be nearer, wouldn't we?'

'What does Simon say?'

'I'm not even bothering to tell him,' said Elaine, the frost creeping into her voice. 'He's been elusive lately anyway. Think he's been seeing Ros. She's welcome. He'll be gone before she knows it, and good riddance.'

'Nothing like a new romance to put a sparkle in your life.'

'You mean me and Neil?' Elaine laughed. 'We'll see. Give you a ring after my interview! Cheers.'

Nicola went back to Iris. 'She's on a high. I think romance beckons again.'

'*That* old business. Think I'll stick with my kibbutz plan. It's got to be more exciting than Joe,' returned Iris with a tragi-comic expression.

Sunday was another warm day. Nicola dressed in a soft green cotton sundress for the afternoon outing. The sleek blue car was there waiting when she went downstairs, with Chrissie already sitting in the front seat alongside Alex. He got out to open the back door.

Chrissie turned round. 'Hi!' she said brightly. 'Ooh! I do like your dress. Mummy said I should have put on something decent.' She was wearing blue shorts and a matching T-shirt, her pony-tail tied back with a blue ribbon.

'You'll do,' Alex said, himself in casual gear.

'You've seen your mummy, have you?' asked Nicola as they set off. 'How is she?'

'She's all right. I say, fancy her being pregnant! I wouldn't have minded. She'd have had to stay home then, wouldn't she, and I could've left school. I had a dreadful night when I first heard she was in hospital. Well, I mean in bed in hospital, as opposed to working there. I imagined her dying and me being an orphan. Can you be an orphan with one parent, Alex?'

'Half an orphan I suppose.'

'Well, I cried for hours and hours. I thought how sorry everyone would be for me if I were an orphan.'

'What a morbid young lady you are,' Alex teased.

'I know. I love sad things, don't you, Nicky? Like *Love Story*, when the heroine died. And *Romeo and Juliet* . . . I mean, how awful to wake up and find your lover has killed himself.'

Nicola caught Alex's eye in the driving mirror. She managed to smile back at him in spite of that innocent reminder of her own past. 'I prefer happy endings,' she said. 'Where are we bound for?'

'He won't say. He's in one of his mysterious moods. Isn't he a beast?'

'I'll tell you this,' said Alex, as he steered the car through leafy Leicestershire lanes, 'you're going to work for your tea this afternoon. You too, Nicola.'

She sat back and enjoyed the passing scene. Lacy cow's parsley waved by the roadside. Trees overhung the winding roads, filtering the sunlight. Buttercups glowed on a gentle rise.

Driving through a quiet village where thatched cottages rambled down one side of the road, Alex took a left-hand turn into a narrow lane which cut through a meadow. A notice-board at the entrance read—Hillside Farm. Accredited Friesian Herd. The black-and-white cows standing placidly chewing the cud were a credit to their owner.

'Oh! Are we going to the farm?' Chrissie said eagerly.

'We are. It belongs to my aunt and uncle. It's my second home really, because I'm a proper orphan, you know.'

A cluster of outbuildings straggled around the mellow, grey stone farmhouse. At the approach of the car the farm dog came barking a warning. Alex pulled up outside. A plump, elderly woman came to the open door, a welcoming smile wreathing her cheeks. She greeted Alex with an affectionate kiss. 'You managed to get away then?'

Nicola and Chrissie stood by waiting to be introduced. 'Come and meet my Aunt Letty,' Alex said. 'She's the best cook in the county.'

'And too fond of my own cooking!' She laughed,

patting her ample hips. 'To think I was once a slip of a girl like you. Nïce to meet you, my dear.' She shook Nicola by the hand before turning her attention to Chrissie. 'I see you're all dressed for climbing trees, then?'

'Climbing trees?'

'Yes, didn't Alex tell you? They're picking the cherries today. We can always do with extra help.'

'Oh, super!' Chrissie's eyes sparkled. 'I *love* cherries.'

'The idea is to pick them, not eat them,' said Alex, flicking her pony-tail.

Aunt Letty smiled. 'I daresay we shan't miss what you can eat. Now come inside and have a nice cold drink first.' She led the way into a large, comfortable kitchen where a ginger cat lay stretched out on a rug in front of the Aga. In a box close by were half a dozen day-old chicks, balls of yellow fluff.

'Oh! Aren't they sweet?' Chrissie knelt down beside them. 'May I pick one up?'

'Yes, do. I bought them in the market yesterday. I'm going to rear them.' Aunt Letty produced cans of cold drinks from the outsized fridge and set tumblers on the table. 'Sit down, dears, and help yourselves.'

The aunt obviously had a very soft spot for this nephew. She treated him like a well-loved son. And it was evident by her sideways glances and questions that she was more than a little intrigued by Nicola's presence.

'Nicola works with me in orthopaedics,' Alex explained, 'although we *have* been known to cross swords,' he added with a sly grin.

'Ah! Stands up for herself, does she? Good for you, my girl.'

'Don't encourage her, Letty. She's bolshie enough.'

'I'm not,' returned Nicola, 'I have opinions of my own, that's all.'

Chrissie took a long guzzle of Coke. 'My mother says . . .' She stopped and put a hand to her mouth.

'And what does your mother say?' prompted Alex.

'That I should keep my mouth shut,' returned Chrissie with a giggle.

The farmer arrived, bringing with him a country smell of fresh air and hay. It was easy to see where the relationship lay. He was as tall as Alex, his fair complexion weathered by the open-air life and his thick hair prematurely white.

'Where's all this help I'm supposed to be getting?' he boomed. 'Hallo, m'boy.' He shook hands with Alex. There were introductions and an exchange of pleasantries before they followed him out into the cherry orchard. Ladders were set against trees, the boughs of which drooped with heavy crops of ripe fruits. 'It's a bumper harvest this year, thanks to my patent bird scarers,' said the farmer.

In sharp contrast to their normal way of life, the visitors spent an enjoyable afternoon picking and boxing. Chrissie was up and down ladders like a squirrel, her ears hung with cherry couplets. Nicola collected baskets and tipped the contents into waiting boxes. When it was time to call a halt they all collapsed on the grass, tired but exhilarated.

Presently Chrissie went away with the farmer to

see a new baby calf and Aunt Letty went indoors to get tea. Alex rolled over onto his stomach and tickled Nicola under the chin with a clover bloom. She had been lying on her back with her eyes closed, hands behind her head. The air was soft. The world seemed far away. And the man beside her, he was like the prince of a fairy story, strong, kind and handsome. A pity he was so utterly exasperating. She opened her eyes to find him looking down at her, propped up on one elbow.

'What were you dreaming about?' he said.

'Oh, nothing really.'

'It must have been a pleasant nothing by the look on your face.'

His studied scrutiny sent a tingle of excitement through her veins. She felt her colour rise and sat up to break the simmering undercurrent that flowed between them. 'Gosh!' she said. 'My hands are filthy.'

He glanced at his own. 'Yes, we'd better get washed.' Rising to his feet in one easy movement, he held out his hands to her and pulled her up.

They were in intimate contact, the warmth of his body seeping through the thin cotton of her dress. Her heart hammered painfully as he held onto her far longer than was necessary, his eyes seeking hers. She felt she could conceal nothing from that penetrating gaze. He could see right through her. He was well aware of the way his touch affected her.

She looked away, stepping back to escape his hold. With a wry smile he tucked an arm about her waist and strolled with her back to the farmhouse.

After an enormous tea they left to take Chrissie back to school.

Letty waved them goodbye. 'Don't make it so long next time, Alex. And bring Nicola to see us again sometime.'

'I'm exhausted,' Chrissie yawned when they delivered her back to the convent complete with a large bag of cherries to share with her friends. 'But it was a gorgeous surprise, Alex. Bye.' And she reached her arms up and kissed him enthusiastically.

Alex and Nicola sped back towards the town. 'Now, that was what I call a proper reward for my efforts,' he said. 'Are you going to express your appreciation in the same way?'

She smiled. 'It might be misinterpreted, in a bigger girl.'

'Good heavens! You didn't bite my head off this time. Must be the civilising influence of rural life.'

'They're nice people, your aunt and uncle. Do they have any family?'

'No, only me.'

The car purred sweetly on its way. 'So you're having a spell of nights,' he remarked. 'When do you start?'

'Tomorrow. I quite like nights. The only trouble is you lose touch with friends a bit.'

A motor-cyclist with a girl on the pillion overtook them at speed, beating the traffic lights as they turned to red. 'Mad fool,' muttered Alex, braking.

It happened a split second after that. A car shot from the side-road and hit the motor cycle broadside. The pillion rider was flung into the air. Nicola gasped. Alex let out an oath. 'C'mon—better see what we can do.'

Hastily they unbelted and she ran with him to the scene of the crash.

The driver of the car, a middle-aged man, got out. He was ashen-faced and shaking. 'Oh, God! I never even saw him . . .'

The motor-cyclist lay trapped beneath the heavy machine. 'Help me get this off,' Alex urged the man.

Nicola had gone to help the other victim. The girl raised herself on one elbow. She looked dazed.

'Don't try to move, love. Let's take your helmet off. Did you hit your head?'

'N-no, I don't think so . . . m-my leg . . .'

Her foot was lying at an abnormal angle. Her jeans had been ripped with the impact. There was a dark stain of blood seeping into the material. Nicola put a supportive arm around the girl's shoulders. 'My friend's a doctor and he'll be with us in a minute, when he's finished seeing to your friend. What's your name?'

'Muriel White. How's Trevor? He's not?' Her eyes were large with fear.

Nicola glanced across. 'Don't worry, my friend's looking after him.'

Other traffic had stopped and a knot of by-standers collected. One went to call an ambulance.

Having done what he could for the boy, Alex came over and knelt beside the girl, his eyes assessing her injuries. 'Are you in much pain?'

She shook her head. 'I-it's not too bad.'

'Help's on its way—won't be long now,' he said in a soothing voice.

She nodded towards her boyfriend. 'H-how's he?'

'No broken bones as far as I can tell. You probably took most of the impact on your leg. But he's knocked himself out.'

Her face crumpled. 'W-we were getting married next week . . .'

With a wail of its klaxon the ambulance arrived. The team brought their stretchers and equipment. One of the men recognised Alex. 'Hallo, sir. More customers for you? Fellow's in pretty bad shape, by the look of it,' he muttered.

'Yes. Signs of cerebral compression. Probably a fractured skull. You're taking them to Priory Cross? Tell them I'm on my way.'

A police car screeched up as the ambulance took off with the casualties, and after giving his statement Alex and Nicola went back to the car.

'Poor kids,' she said. 'I can't see there being any wedding next week.'

'No, neither can I. Oh well, back to work.' He gave a twisted smile. 'I had hoped to finish the day on a brighter note, since you like happy endings.'

'I'm beginning to wonder if they exist in real life.'

'Don't be a pessimist. We have our successes as well as our failures, don't we?' he consoled.

'Yes, but . . .'

'But what?'

She shrugged. 'Oh, nothing.'

They had reached the hospital now and he pulled up outside the A and E wing. She got out of the car. 'I hope you can patch them up anyway. Good luck.'

Going across to her room she was in sombre

mood. Another couple of lives blighted. She hoped
they could save the girl's leg. It had looked a mess.
As for the boy, his future was anyone's guess.

CHAPTER NINE

CLOSING her curtains on Monday afternoon, Nicola went to bed to catch a few hours' sleep before going on duty at nine o'clock that night. Since her outing to the farm she had done a lot of thinking, mostly about Alex. Although he appeared to have guessed what was in her mind, he had made no attempt to explain the situation between himself and Dora. But that was typical of the man. To justify himself to anyone would be against his principles. You accepted him for what he was or you could go to hell.

She began to ask herself the question he had thrown at her. *Had* she seen Dora as some kind of threat? Alex did have a certain magnetism which she found compelling. He had only to look at her in a certain way and disturbing sensations coursed through her body. But that was only his undeniable physical attraction, wasn't it? How could she feel threatened when she had no desire whatsoever to start another love affair? She didn't intend ever to be hurt again. And she would be a fool to think of him in those terms in any case. He treated her with the same half-humorous patronage that he extended to Chrissie or any other waif and stray.

That was the end of the matter. She would think no more about it. Finally she slept but when she awoke he was still there at the back of her brain, ripping her resolution to pieces. She realised she

170

was going to miss him during her period of nights.
Apart from emergencies he was scarcely likely to
be around in the small hours.

There were two other nurses on duty with
Nicola. Yvonne, a third year, and Tricia, a
married SEN. Jean Arden gave them the handover report.

'There was a road traffic accident admitted
on Sunday evening. Muriel White, nineteen,
compound fractures of tib and fib.'

'She came to us, did she? I was there when it
happened.'

'What do you mean, you were there?' said Jean.

'We'd taken Dora's daughter out for the afternoon and we were on the way back.'

'Oh! Well, the leg's a bit of a mess. She's going to
need skin grafts later.'

'The fellow who was with her, do you know how
he is?'

'In ITU on a life-support machine.'

'Oh dear. But I'm not surprised,' said Nicola.
'Does she know?'

Jean shrugged. 'I don't know exactly what she's
been told. She seems pretty depressed. Anyway,
she's on traction with a Steinmann's pin. We put
her in with young Avril. Thought it might help—
two young ones together with similar injuries.'

After giving details of the rest of the patients,
Jean concluded, 'Bridget's gone home, and Sister
Flint's also gone, so the side ward's empty. We're
on take tonight. Hope you're not too busy. Night-
night.' And she departed with the rest of the day
staff.

Nicola's two companions were already familiar

with the patients, having been on the previous night. Yvonne started the late night drinks while Tricia busied herself with the TPR's.

Before starting the drugs round Nicola went to see Murial. 'Hallo! Remember me?' she said with a sympathetic smile.

Muriel looked at her blankly for a moment; then recognition dawned. 'Oh! Oh yes,' she said, 'You were there when we crashed. You look different in uniform.'

'I expect I do. How are you feeling?'

The girl sighed heavily. There were high spots of colour on her cheeks and her temperature chart showed erratic peaks and troughs. 'My leg feels pretty awful.'

'Never mind. I'll be coming with your pain-killer in a minute, then you'll be able to get some sleep.'

Muriel caught her hand as she turned to go. 'They won't tell me how Trevor is. Do you know?'

'Well, only that he's in intensive care.' Nicola looked across to the other bed. 'Avril's boyfriend was in ITU for a while after their accident. He's all right now, isn't he?'

Avril nodded, waved to the other girl and scribbled a message on her pad. Nicola passed it over and left the two to communicate.

By eleven p.m. all the drugs and injections had been given, transfusions checked, pillows made comfortable, last bedpans and bottles given out and patients settled for the night. The ward lights were dimmed and the one over the nurses' station lowered.

But it was midnight before the staff had completed their tidying up. They relaxed together in the office over the first cup of coffee.

Tricia yawned. 'Hope it's quieter tonight. Last night Alex Baron was here till all hours dealing with that new girl. Then when he'd gone we had to get Max out of bed because Mr Armstrong started having chest pains. It turned out to be indigestion, thank goodness.'

'Well, at least it stopped you dropping off,' grinned Nicola.

'Nurse!' came a hoarse whisper from Mr Armstrong's bed.

'Oh no! Not more chest pains!' She hurried to investigate.

'Sorry to trouble you, love. I need a bottle. Must've been asleep when they came round.'

'OK,' said Nicola with a sigh of relief, 'I'll get you one.'

Night Sister arrived to do her round and later they took turns to have their meal break. There were no undue disturbances. The small hours passed tediously in between the occasional checks to see that all was well with the patients. Yvonne tried to do some revision, Tricia took out a sweater she was knitting for her husband, and Nicola browsed over the daily paper she had borrowed from someone.

By five-thirty some of the patients had begun to stir and the busy work of the morning could begin. Yvonne took round the morning tea while Nicola and Tricia washed some of the less able patients and made their beds. There were countless other jobs to be carried out but all was completed in time and by seven-thirty Nicola was ready to give her report. She went off duty glad to have her first night over.

The week continued in much the same uneventful pattern. There were only routine admissions and discharges and no crises. Muriel's pyrexia was responding to antibiotics and the sepsis in her wounds was under control. Her mental state, however, was less satisfactory. She was often to be found quietly weeping. Even with sedatives she was restless during the night and all the nurses made efforts trying to cheer her up.

On Friday the orderly pattern of the ward was broken. The night staff arrived to find the day work running late. Two road traffic accidents had been admitted straight from theatre, the last of which had just been brought in.

'Sorry, we're all behind,' Jean said, 'and old Mr Day has just had an accident in the bed. He seems a bit confused.'

'All right, don't you worry, we'll see to him,' said Nicola.

'Will you? Thanks. The two new admissions are on half-hourly obs. And they're both on whole blood. There's more in the fridge . . . both AB positive.' She went on to give the rest of the report, concluding, 'By the way, they switched off the life-support machine of Muriel's boyfriend.'

'Oh, my God! That's awful,' said Nicola. 'Does she know?'

'Yes. Her mother told her. Well, she had to be told some time or other.'

'How did she take it?'

'Quietly, as a matter of fact. No histrionics.' Jean gathered up her belongings. 'I'll be off then.'

The night nurses flew around the ward endeavouring to catch up with the work. Nicola checked first on the new patients before helping Tricia to change Mr Day's bed; he certainly did seem disorientated.

They then started the ten o'clock drug round together. Handing Muriel her pills and pouring her a glass of water, Nicola said, 'I heard about Trevor . . . I'm so very sorry. Perhaps it was for the best though.'

'That's what they all say,' returned the girl flatly. She swallowed her medication and handed back the glass.

'At least he didn't suffer, Muriel. He wouldn't have known much about anything from the time it happened.'

'I suppose that's something to be thankful for. Will you get my handbag out of the locker before you go?'

Nicola found the bag and passed it to her. Tricia raised her eyebrows as they moved on. 'Seems to have accepted it all right,' she murmured.

'Do you think so? I don't know.' Nicola had an eerie feeling that it was too good to be true.

They had more or less caught up with the work when Yvonne, checking on one of the new patients, reported that his drip seemed to have tissued. Nicola tried to restart it but no amount of fiddling would get it flowing again. She sighed. 'We'll have to bleep Night Sister.'

Night Sister duly came, but she also was unable to put matters right. 'I'll have to get the houseman. It's Mr Baron's team on—I think they're still in theatre.' She called the theatre and Max O'Malley sent a message to say he'd be along as soon as he was free.

'While you're here, Sister,' Nicola said, 'will you have a look at Mr Day? He's a hip replacement. He's complaining of a headache and he's uncharacteristically irritable and a bit vague.'

They walked down the ward together. They found the patient very restless and tetchy. 'You've got a headache, Mr Day?' Sister said.

'Yes, I have. Shouldn't't've sat in the sun . . . this pillow's solid rock . . .' He burbled something else they couldn't understand.

'Doctor will be along in a minute. We'll get him to give you something for the pain,' Night Sister promised.

They shook up the pillow and turned it over for him. Sister frowned as they left him. 'His speech sounds slurred, doesn't it? Get Max to have a look at him when he comes. He might have had a slight stroke. And better put up some cot sides, don't want him falling out of bed.'

It was two a.m. when Max arrived. Although weary he was still his affable self. 'Just finished our third emergency tonight. Don't worry, it's going to Jones Ward. Now, what can I do for you?'

'That last new admission's drip has stopped,' Nicola explained, taking him along to the patient.

'Oh, that'll need resiting,' Max decided. She brought a fresh sterile pack and within a few minutes he had the difficulty sorted out.

'Sorry to keep you, Max,' Nicola apologised, 'but Mr Day's behaving rather oddly—will you have a look at him?'

'Sure.' After carrying out a neurological examination, asking a number of questions and noting certain symptoms, Max said, 'We'll give you something for the headache now Mr Day and have a proper look at you in the morning.'

Walking back to the office with Nicola he confirmed Night Sister's suspicions. 'Yes, it's probably a slight CVA—some weakness on the left side. Have you got the BNF? I'll see what I can give him.'

He looked up a suitable tranquiliser in the standard drug list and wrote it up on the medication chart. 'There you are. Is that the lot?'

'Yes, thank you Max. We'll try not to worry you again. You must be dead on your feet.'

He made a wry face. 'I should've joined the church like my mother wanted me to!' and with a cheery wave he ambled away.

Nicola gave Mr Day his injection. Things quietened down. Yvonne went for her meal break and Night Sister returned to check that the doctor had been. 'You're all right now then?' she said, and continued her round.

Tricia went to make more coffee. Nicola put her feet on the waste-paper basket and began to write up the events of the night so far. Her thoughts wandered to Alex, beavering away in theatre for the second night in succession. And the more she thought about him the more she realised that he had slowly and subtley taken a hold on her affections. Well, you could be fond of a person without wanting to get involved with him. For instance, she was fond of Max. But deep in her heart, although she was loathe to admit it, she knew her feelings for the dynamic registrar went a great deal deeper than that.

Tricia brought in the coffee and they both relaxed. Nicola yawned, rubbed her eyes and stretched. 'Thank goodness I'm nights off after this . . .' she began, when a muffled cry from down the ward made them both start.

'What was that?' frowned Tricia.

Avril's light began flashing. 'Nurse!' The frightened voice came from the direction of her bay.

Other muffled sounds of distress reached their ears. They hurried with a torch to see what was wrong. Her eyes large and scared, Avril pointed towards Muriel. She was jabbing wildly at her wrist with a pair of pointed nail scissors, trying to stifle her cries as she hurt herself.

Nicola grabbed the wrist and fought to take the scissors from the demented girl. With the strength of despair she struck out at the nurses as well as herself. 'Don't! Don't!' she wailed, 'Let me die! Let me die!'

They managed at last to overpower her and wrest the scissors from her clenched fingers. Nicola pressed the panic button to summon assistance from Jones Ward. 'I've got her, Trish,' she said, maintaining a firm pressure on the girl's bleeding wrist. 'Go and bleep Night Sister.'

Muriel sank back against her pillow, her body shaking with deep convulsive sobs, all resistance gone. 'Oh God! Why did you stop me? He's gone, he's gone!'

'Hush, my love.' Nicola held the girl tight in her arms, trying to find words of comfort. 'I know it's bad, but you'll feel better in the morning.' This was no time for instant pep talks, she knew. Life was always at its lowest ebb in the small hours.

'I can't live without him! I can't!' wept Muriel.

'Yes, you can. He wouldn't want you to waste your life, would he?' Still keeping pressure on the bleeding wrist, she let the girl's grief exhaust itself in deep, shuddering tears.

Rapid feet signalled that help was at hand. Alex, who had been in Jones Ward, strode into the bay with Tricia hurrying to keep up as she put him in the picture. The registrar had been stretched to capacity that night. His lean face was taut, his blue eyes dark with strain. Yet he was brisk and professional, still managing to dredge up reserves of patience and energy from some remote source.

'Let me see, Muriel,' he said, his deep voice quite calm as he took the damaged wrist in his hands. 'Ah! Not too bad. A couple of stitches should do it.' He nodded to Nicola to get a suture pack. 'And we'll have ten mgs Diazepam IV please.' He sat on the side of the bed talking quietly to the girl while the nurses went to carry out his orders.

Night Sister appeared and swished the curtains around the bed. Alex put the tranquilliser into a vein before cleaning up and suturing the gash in Muriel's wrist. Fortunately she had not managed to pierce a large blood vessel and presently, the drug acting quickly, she became subdued.

'Now you go to sleep and it'll all look different in the morning. When you touch bottom there's only one way to go and that's up again.' The doctor went back to the office with Night Sister to make out an incident report.

Tricia and Nicola stayed to tidy the bed and sponge Muriel's face and hands. She was becoming increasingly drowsy as they pulled back the curtains.

Avril was watching, wide-eyed. 'I-is she . . . all right?'

Nicola nodded. Then she paused, her mouth gaping. 'Avril, you spoke!' she said.

'Yes . . . I did.' There was a wondering smile on Avril's face.

'Well, well! That's the one bright spot tonight. They said it would happen suddenly, didn't they?'

The nurses beamed at each other. Tricia wheeled away the equipment and Nicola went to the sink to wash. Her hands and arms still bore signs of her tussle with Muriel. Turning on the tap she rinsed off the dried blood. Her forearm was sore. She knew the scissors had caught her but she didn't realise how deeply until then. Washing the place started the bleeding afresh.

She showed the wound to Tricia, who frowned and insisted on her showing it to Alex.

'Nicola's been cut,' she announced in the office.

The registrar looked up sharply. He came to examine the wound. 'That needs a stitch. When did you last have an anti-tetanus jab?'

'A-about six months ago, I think.'

'Come on, I'll give you a booster.' He hustled her out of the office into the treatment room. Her limbs felt suddenly trembly and she sat down abruptly on a chair.

Night Sister bustled in to help. She fixed a plaster over the wound when it had been pulled together with silk. 'Are you feeling all right, dear? You look a bit pale. Would you like to go off?'

'Good heavens, no,' protested Nicola. 'It's only a scratch. I'm fine.'

Alex gave a one-sided smile. 'She's much too stubborn to give in. Perhaps she could have a night off tomorrow?'

'I'm off anyway,' Nicola said.

'Good. Have a day in bed,' returned Alex.

Someone bleeped for Night Sister at that point and she left them together.

He eyed her steadily. 'You've had quite a night of it.'

'So have you.' She sighed and looked pensive. 'Poor Muriel. I know what she must have been going through.'

'Do you?' His perceptive blue eyes bored into her. 'You must tell me about it when I'm in a better state to listen.' He paused. 'I meant what I said . . . about that day in bed.'

'You've no control over my off-duty,' she said with a negative half-smile.

'You'll do as you're told. Must I come and check up on you?'

'Don't bully me.'

He said nothing, continuing to look at her in a way that threatened her carefully preserved self-control. She was relieved when he left to catch up on some sleep himself.

The rest of the night passed without further drama and they were all heartily glad when it was time to hand over to the day staff.

'My feet are ready to drop off,' groaned Tricia as they left the ward.

Nicola's body ached with weariness. Her throat felt tight with emotion. She fell straight into bed and slept dreamlessly until seven that evening. Waking refreshed and hungry, she put on her dressing-gown, made herself a sandwich and ate it alone in front of Iris's television.

Iris joined her when she came off duty at nine-thirty that evening. They had an hour together, talking over the crisis on Montfort Ward until, overcome with sleep again, Nicola went off once more to her bed.

She felt strangely tranquil. More at peace with herself than she had done for months. In an odd sort of way the things she had said to Muriel had opened her eyes to her own release. Time did heal. You did not forget the bad things but as the months went by you learned acceptance.

In his note Leo had said that she should forget him and be happy. Forget him she never would. But she knew she was ready to start living again. Her heart had not died with Leo as she had first thought. It was like having a great weight lifted from her shoulders.

As had happened so often of late, Alex was there invading her mind. She smiled to herself as she realised she had done as he ordered. For all his abrasive, dictatorial manner, his audacity, he was warm and caring . . . not the villain she had tried to make herself believe. And was there just a hint that it wasn't only her physical well-being that concerned him?

CHAPTER TEN

ON SUNDAY morning Nicola rose late. She had a lazy breakfast in her dressing-gown before penning a long-overdue but cheerful letter to her parents. She felt curiously optimistic, as though on the brink of some great adventure. As she sealed her letter there came a knock on her door. It could only be Iris. 'Come in!' she called.

But it was not Iris. The person who lounged there in the doorway, elegant as ever in well-tailored casual trousers, a short-sleeved fawn sports shirt hugging his broad chest, was Alex.

'H-hallo!' she said, her pulse rate doubling. She pulled her dressing-gown together. 'How did you know where to find me?'

'I asked the warden, of course. How are you?' His shrewd blue eyes assessed her and elemental forces threatened her struggle for composure.

She drew a steadying breath before answering. 'Fine! I've been sleeping practically ever since I came off duty. How's Muriel?'

'She's holding her own. The padre had a yarn with her and Max has got a good line in philosophy, too.'

'You didn't do so badly yourself,' smiled Nicola.

He shrugged. 'Sympathy's cheap. The real healing has to come from within.'

They were both silent for a moment, then he went on. 'What are you doing with yourself today?'

'Nothing much. Being generally lazy.'

'I'm not on call. Let's be lazy together. Get your clothes on and I'll take you on another Alex Baron mystery tour.'

She grinned. 'Another treat for Chrissie?'

'No. A treat for Alex. Get a move on. See you downstairs in half-an-hour.'

When he had left her she felt fluttery with excitement as she tried to decide what to wear. She settled on a pair of white stretch jeans and a striped T-shirt, applied a minimum of make-up, ran a comb through her short brown locks, grabbed a lightweight jacket and went down in the lift to join him.

It was a perfect English summer's day, the sky a high blue vault with just a few banners of white, wispy cloud. This time Alex followed the route towards Warwickshire. Green and lovely meadows were dotted with newly-shorn sheep and wild roses ran riot in the hedgerows.

'We're going to Warwick Castle?' she said.

He maintained his secret smile. 'I said this was a lazy day, not an educational tour. Well, it's not all doom and gloom on Montfort, is it?' he went on.

'You mean, Avril getting her voice back?'

'Well, that too. But haven't you heard about the latest romance?'

'Who? Max and Meryl?'

'Oh, I don't know anything about them. I meant Sister Flint.'

'She's never agreed to saddle herself with that wretch Tresilian?' exclaimed Nicola in disgust.

'No. Arthur has pipped him at the post.'

Nicola laughed. 'Oh, that's terrific! He'll be good

for her. I think she liked the way he bossed her around.'

He gave a lazy smile. 'Does that apply to all women?'

'Well, you've got a head start in that case,' she said.

'All right, come on. You were going to tell me about that skeleton in your cupboard. Let's have it. Have you finally given that fellow the old heave-ho?'

Nicola shook her head and smiled ruefully. 'I said you'd got it wrong. He was just a nuisance.' She found that now she could talk about the tragedy and it didn't hurt so much.

'It was eighteen months ago now—my boyfriend committed suicide.' She couldn't go on for a moment, remembering that dreadful morning when she had found Leo slumped over the wheel of his car.

There was a stunned silence. Alex's blithe expression changed. His voice lost its cheerfulness. 'My God!' he said quietly. 'What can I say?' He laid a hand over hers. 'Don't talk about it if you'd rather not.'

'I—it's all right. I want to tell you. It's a relief in a way.'

The story began to pour out of her in a disjointed fashion. 'Leo worked in a bank. We were as close as two people could be, or so I thought. What I didn't know was that he was a compulsive gambler. Horses, gaming clubs, fruit machines . . . anything. He borrowed money from me sometimes, but I simply thought he'd run out of cash.' She swallowed and picked at her nails. 'He got involved with

money-lenders—started diverting cheques to his
own account at the bank to pay them off. It came to
light . . . he couldn't face the consequences. I
found him . . . in the garage, in his car. Carbon
monoxide poisoning. It was horrible.' She shud-
dered and covered her face with her hands as if to
shut out the memory. 'I felt guilty to be alive. I
should have known, might have helped him.'

Alex had listened in silence, his eyes full of pain
for her. He shook his head in self-reproach. 'I'm an
idiot—I never guessed it was anything like that.'

'It's all right. I'm over it now.'

'Are you really?' His brow furrowed anxiously.

'Yes, and I'm glad you know.'

They were both quiet for a while. Then she said:
'Why didn't you tell me about Dora's husband?'

'Oh! You know about that, do you?'

Nicola nodded. 'She told me. You shouldn't
have let me think . . .'

'It wasn't *my* secret to tell, was it? Besides, why
should *you* have cared if you thought we were
sleeping around?' A lighter note crept into his
voice, and he flung her a sideways smile.

She didn't answer. She felt he knew why.

'He'll be out of the clinic by the time she's home,'
Alex went on. 'He's a decent guy when he's not
hitting the bottle.' He paused. 'So my slate's wiped
clean now, is it?'

'Pure as the driven snow!' she said, determinedly
shutting out memories of the past.

'Snow's not that pure. Stir it with your boot and
you never know what you'll find. There's a hotbed
of fiendish cunning beneath this innocent exterior.'

They had reached the outskirts of a town, passing

a large notice board which said 'Welcome to Royal
Leamington Spa'.'

'Ever been here before?' he asked.

'No.' She looked around with interest at elegant
Victorian houses, spaciously laid out.

'You'll like it.' The quiet, leisurely town had a
holiday atmosphere. Driving along past beautifully
laid out gardens, Alex turned in at an imposing
country club where they stopped for lunch.

There were snowy cloths with garden roses on
the tables and deferential, white-jacketed waiters
to serve the excellent bill of fare. He ordered
champagne to accompany their lunch.

'Are we celebrating something?' she said.

'Yes, I think you might say that.' But he didn't
explain what.

She stirred her coffee at the end of the meal.
'That was lovely, Alex. A taste of gracious living.'

'Makes a welcome change from the hospital canteen, doesn't it?' He watched her lazily. His eyes
held a message that had nothing to do with food.
She glanced away, her colour deepening. 'A liber-
ated woman who still blushes?' he said.

She curbed a smile and fanned her cheeks with
the menu. 'It's the coffee.'

He laughed and beckoned the waiter. 'Come on,'
he said after settling the bill, 'perhaps a blow on the
river will cool you down. Although I doubt whether
it will me.' Putting an arm round her waist he
walked her back to the car.

A short drive brought them back to the riverside
gardens. It was a lovely stretch of water, willow-
lined, with ducks sunning themselves on the banks
and a pair of swans gliding in stately splendour.

Taking her hand he made for the landing-stage where boats waited to be hired.

'Oh, I haven't been in a rowing-boat since I was a kid,' she said, bright-eyed.

'Nothing so restorative as being afloat.' He steadied the craft while she stepped in. Settling back against her seat, she watched the muscles rippling in his strong arms as he manoeuvred the oars to take the boat out into midstream.

They were soon beyond the formal gardens and into the meadow-banked reach where the willows formed shady arbours with their overhanging branches.

He drew into the bank under one of the trees and shipped the oars. He patted the seat beside him and crooked his forefinger at her. 'Come over here, you tantalising water-sprite.'

The boat wobbled slightly as she rose. 'Will it be safe?'

'Do you mean from falling in . . . or from me?'

'Both.'

'No guarantees.' He reached out a hand to her. 'The former controls the latter, to a certain extent.'

When she was safely nestled in the crook of his arm he murmured against her hair. 'I want you, you know that, don't you? I've loved you from the moment I saw you snivelling in the corner of that railway carriage. I wanted to take you in my arms and cuddle you. I wanted to kiss that ridiculous pink nose and those wobbly lips.'

'But you said goodbye at the station,' she protested. 'You didn't know we should ever meet again.'

'Oh, yes I did. With Priory Cross Hospital on

your luggage-label and a nursing magazine on your lap? Do you think I'd have let you out of my sight otherwise? You've kept me waiting, but I knew I should win in the end.'

'You did, did you?' She reached up and gave him a fleeting kiss.

'Aha! So I didn't need to buy one, did I? But I'm sure we can do better than that.' His arms drew her close. His mouth sought hers. The water lapped gently against the boat and in their green bower Alex caressed her, possessively, persuasively. Desire welled up within her. It was almost too much to bear, the potent power of his loving.

'Oh, Alex!' she murmured, returning kiss for kiss.

'Oh, Nicola,' he returned, pressing a finger on her nose. 'Do I take it this is to your liking?'

'Don't ask silly questions.' She pulled his face to hers again.

His lips were gently probing at first, becoming more passionate as she submitted freely to his demands. For a while there was no sound save the soft movement of the river against the side of the boat.

Presently they drew a little apart. He lifted her hand and kissed each finger in turn. His eyes gazing intently into hers held her captive. 'Woman, you drive me to distraction. Perhaps I'll lock you up at home to keep you all to myself.'

Her senses throbbed with longing but she made a valiant attempt to sound in control.

'You're living in the wrong age. Women aren't chattels any more.'

'My darling! My darling!' he said in mock despair, 'Promise you'll make an honest man of me! If you don't I shall shrivel away to a handful of dust, here and now, before your very eyes. And you'll have to row yourself back.'

The sun was shining through the branches, lighting up his thick fair hair. Her sun-god threatening to disintegrate? She couldn't allow that to happen.

'Well?' he demanded. 'Do you promise?'

Her lips twitched. 'Is that a proposal?'

'More like an ultimatum. I'm not taking no for an answer.'

'I . . .' But that was as far as she got because it was impossible to talk when he was kissing her as if there were no tomorrow . . .

4 Doctor Nurse Romances
FREE

Coping with the daily tragedies and ordeals of a busy hospital, and sharing the satisfaction of a difficult job well done, people find themselves unexpectedly drawn together. Mills & Boon Doctor Nurse Romances capture perfectly the excitement, the intrigue and the emotions of modern medicine, that so often lead to overwhelming and blissful love. By becoming a regular reader of Mills & Boon Doctor Nurse Romances you can enjoy EIGHT superb new titles every two months plus a whole range of special benefits: your very own personal membership card, a free newsletter packed with recipes, competitions, bargain book offers, plus big cash savings.

**AND an Introductory FREE GIFT for YOU.
Turn over the page for details.**